Checkin

CHECKING HIM OUT

by
Debbie McGowan

Beaten Track
www.beatentrackpublishing.com

Checking Him Out

First published 2014 by MMRomanceGroup.com (ebook)
Published 2015 Beaten Track Publishing
Copyright © 2014, 2015, 2018 Debbie McGowan

All rights reserved.

No part of this publication may be reproduced, stored in a retrieval system, or transmitted, in any form or by any means, without the prior permission of the publisher, nor be otherwise circulated without the publisher's prior consent in any form of binding or cover other than that in which it is published and without a similar condition including this condition being imposed on the subsequent publisher.

The moral right of the author has been asserted.

ISBN: 978 1 910635 02 5

Song Lyrics (public domain):
"It Takes A Little Rain With The Sunshine
To Make The World Go Round"
– Words by Ballard MacDonald / Music by Harry Carroll, 1913.

Cover:
Background image: "His Hand, The Sun" by Giovanni Dall'Orto –
commons.wikimedia.org/wiki/User:G.dallorto
Foreground image: licensed stock image - usage is not indicative of the model's identity, activities or preferences.

Beaten Track Publishing,
Burscough. Lancashire.
www.beatentrackpublishing.com

Acknowledgements

I am eternally indebted to my beta/proofreaders:

Larry Benjamin, fabulous author and tough cookie, evidently seeking his revenge for our past editing bust-ups;

My old faithfuls, Nige and Trace;

K.C. Faelan, who fit/fitted in beta-reading and educated me along the way;

Shayla Mist, for making me feel amazing!

Rick Bettencourt, for all things Boston, and for not mocking/sharing an, um, eye for detail.

Thank you also to the M/M Romance Group in general, and the mods in particular, for your support, patience and humor. You are truly wonderful.

Finally, a huge thanks to Taya, for the brilliant and inspiring prompt, and your ongoing encouragement. I hope I did it justice.

NOTE: This story was first published as part of the Love's Landscapes Anthology (DRiTC 2014, MMRomanceGroup.com),

based on a prompt, which you can read here: www.mmromancegroup.com/checking-him-out-by-debbie-mcgowan/

***

This novel is a work of fiction and the characters and events in it exist only in its pages and in the author's imagination.

Content advisory: this story contains sex acts between consenting male adults.

Contents

Chapter One 1
Chapter Two 7
Chapter Three 13
Chapter Four 19
Chapter Five 25
Chapter Six 33
Chapter Seven 45
Chapter Eight 53
Chapter Nine 59
Chapter Ten 67
Chapter Eleven 77
Chapter Twelve 85
Chapter Thirteen 95
Chapter Fourteen 105
Chapter Fifteen 113
Chapter Sixteen 119
Chapter Seventeen 133
Chapter Eighteen 145
Chapter Nineteen 153
Chapter Twenty 163

Chapter Twenty-One 171
Chapter Twenty-Two 177
Chapter Twenty-Three 183
Chapter Twenty-Four 193
Epilogue 203
About the Author 209
By the Author 210
Beaten Track Publishing 212

Chapter One

I probably wouldn't have noticed, but the guy was wearing sweatpants with nothing underneath. First the attempt to shove his way behind me, then the hot palm on my shoulder. Elise stopped talking, and all of a sudden I had no idea what she'd been saying.

"Hey, would you mind?" That was Captain Impatient, his crotch now level with my ass, pressing into me, because there's really not enough space in a checkout aisle for two big guys to pass by untouched, though it wasn't the physical contact that threw me.

Captain Impatient.

He was my height, maybe a little shorter, so around six one, and my build—yeah, I work out, a lot. And he was looking right past me, like he was so sure I'd let him go ahead, even though I could take him, in more ways than one. He had a strong, kind of musky scent going on—guess he worked out a lot too, and that's where he'd been. A guy who's got any sense of pride gets a shower first, but not this guy. Probably couldn't wait long enough. His hand was still on my shoulder, the distinctive smell of residual sweat and the metal of weights snaking its way up into my nostrils, the heat coming off his chest radiating right across my back. I could almost taste him. And I could feel him, getting hard inside his sweats…

Elise was about to reply, but I shot him a glance over my shoulder.

We'd been in the store a long time, and I was getting tetchy. Flattered by his reaction, but tetchy nonetheless.

The moment passed. He ground his way back to his place in the line, smiled, far from apologetically, and followed up with, "Sorry. It's just I figured as I only had this, and you're, well…"

His accent. He was British—English, in fact, with a hint of something else—and the words poured off his tongue like maple syrup trickling off hot pancakes. They slid over my skin, pooled around me, stuck my feet to the floor. I was still staring at him. Damn.

I turned back to Elise to find her slamming the last of the groceries onto the belt. She had on her thunderstorm face, the one where her eyes flash with danger and darkness falls, thick and heavy. Maybe not today, and maybe not tomorrow either, but at some point the thunderclap would come, and then the torrential downpour.

Oh boy, was I in trouble.

She left the case of beer in the cart, because there was nowhere else for it to go, and because it was mine. She was making a point of that. She attempted to reconvene the conversation, but I was only aware of her mouth moving. I couldn't hear the words over the blood pumping in my ears. I had my back to him, as he took a call on his cell. I heard that, loud and clear.

"The store on Memorial," he said to person unknown. "Yeah, that's the one. See you in five." A pause. "You too. Bye. Bye."

Pause and confirmation.

Love you.

You too.

That's what it'd be, right? Why should I care? I was a married man. *Happily* married man, so they told me. Maybe I didn't agree with the happy part so much, but I sure as hell wasn't interested in this guy.

"Chrissakes, Sol," Elise hissed.

I snapped myself out of it.

There was space on the belt now, and I effortlessly hoisted the beer, turning as I did so, and caught a brief glimpse of him. Dark hair, short and kind of wavy, square jaw, thick ruddy lips. White sleeveless tee, taut against his chest, picking out, enhancing, defining. A dark tattoo graced his left upper arm, though I couldn't tell what it was. He was counting out the exact money for his purchase—a two-pound tub of vanilla cream protein shake mix. I looked again at our cart-load of groceries, and maybe felt a little mean making him wait. He glanced up, met my gaze. Smiled again.

"You getting this?" Elise asked and opened her purse anyway.

"Uh, yeah. Sure," I said. I moved forward and handed over my card. Sexy guy moved forward too, hot on my tail, and I really do mean on my tail. I wondered if he had personal space issues, as in he was claiming mine. The teller handed my card back. I followed Elise and the cart out to the car.

"You didn't answer my question," she reminded me. I was wondering how much grief I'd get for admitting I had no idea what she'd asked. She saw that I was clueless and sighed so loudly it could have lifted the groceries out of the cart for her. Instead that was left to me. She decided to help me out, with the question, not the groceries. On that score she stood, arms folded, inspecting her nails, watching me heave the multitude of bags into the trunk.

"Rory's party?"

"Right?" I searched my brain for the scattered remnants of what we'd been talking about. It came back to me. Her new boss was having a rooftop garden party, and as husband of the newest junior partner I was expected to attend. I hated those kinds of things—work socials, grocery shopping, anniversary dinners—but that's what I'd signed up for.

"When was it, again?" I asked.

"A week from Thursday. Eight thirty."

I scanned my mental calendar, hoping to find a clash. No joy. I relented with a shrug and we got in the car, drove home in silence and wordlessly stowed the groceries. Elise went to shower. I filled up the coffeemaker, switched it on, but grabbed a beer instead. I was restless, still thinking about him, building him a life story. I'd have said he was single, were it not for the phone conversation. He seemed kind of…available. Interested. Interesting? I guessed he had a physical job, maybe in security, or something, though people made that assumption about me, wrongly. It was crazy. I mean, I'd just met the guy. Not even that much. I'd likely never see him again, and it wasn't as if I was short on options. I considered calling to Elise, to say I was going for a quick workout, see who was still around, but it was getting late and I changed my mind. I turned on the TV, flicked through a few channels. The running shower made for an interesting soundscape to the muted moving slideshow. I took a big gulp of beer and flopped back onto the sofa, immediately rescued from my reluctant R and R by a knock at the door. I automatically checked the time. Nearly ten. I went to answer anyway.

"Hi."

Captain Impatient.

"Hi," I said. He smiled, extending an arm.

"You left this."

I fought to unlock my eyes from his and looked down. My wallet was in his hand.

"Ah. Um, thanks," I uttered inarticulately.

I reached out to take the wallet, my eyes straying down past it. He was no longer in sweatpants. Stonewashed jeans, tan boots. Clean boots. For some reason that irked me. I followed the blue jeans back up, glancing over the smooth black tee. My gaze met his once more, a glistening silvery blue in the glow of light from the apartment, like molten metal. He was still smiling, his mouth a little crooked, tipped up to the left. Infuriatingly, I found myself smiling back. After what seemed an age, my fingers made contact with the wallet. He relinquished his grip on it, though he still had a hold on me, like we were tethered together and neither of us could break away. Finally he nodded and turned to leave.

"Thanks again," I called after him. He raised a hand in acknowledgement. I slowly closed the door, aware of his retreating form, aware of the scent of his cologne on the wallet I was holding. A thought occurred to me.

"Hey! How'd you know where to find me?"

He turned back, raising both hands now in a dismissive shrug.

"Driver's license?"

Duh.

He rounded the corner and disappeared from view. I closed the door, returned to the sofa, carrying my wallet as if it were the most precious gift ever given to me. Elise appeared before me in a short silky floral robe, rubbing her wet hair with a towel.

"Who was that?" she asked.

"The guy from the store." I waved the wallet at her. She looked at me blankly.

"What guy from the store?"

"With the protein shake?"

She nodded once, clearly no clue who I was talking about. "Did you check he didn't take anything?"

"Seriously?"

Oh yeah, she was serious. It wasn't as if I liked him. In fact he'd royally pissed me off, but really, who finds a wallet, loots it, then goes to the effort of returning it? But Elise was unrelenting. I sighed and opened my wallet, trying not to react when I saw what was inside—apart from everything that should be, that is.

"All present and correct," I reported. Elise wandered away, still rubbing her hair.

"I'm going to turn in," she called back.

"OK, hon," I replied.

I waited for our bedroom door to close, quickly typed his number into my cell and disposed of the evidence.

Chapter Two

I woke up the next morning, hard and horny, with the fading memory of an imagined chance meeting at the gym, unimpressed that the anonymous guy of my dreams and fantasies now came complete with a face and identity—no prizes for guessing who. I rolled onto my side and stared at Elise's back. Her alarm was about to go off. Hell, I was about to go off. I could've stayed, got my satisfaction right there in the bed. Instead, I bolted for the bathroom and got in the shower before the temperature stabilized so I could deal with it myself. By the time I emerged, soft and no longer horny, Elise was standing in the doorway, arms folded. I muttered a "good morning" as I passed her. The door closed on me. Now she was pissed too.

I guess I should tell you something about Elise's and my relationship. Give or take a couple of months we were the same age—coming up to thirty-one—and met at college, where she was your all-American girl, studying law—a career girl, you might say, not that her parents agreed with her plans. They made no secret of their hopes to see her "settled down" with a couple of kids, and we hadn't the heart to tell them it just wasn't in the cards.

As for me, I'm from the UK, Britain, England, wherever you want to call it, from a little town in the middle of nowhere. Americans generally think "Britain" is one green and pleasant land, filled with "quaint" little towns of whitewashed cottages, in the middle of which stands London, home of the Queen and the red pillar box. Well, there's a whole gamut of places between those extremes of sprawling metropolis and rural idyll, but where I come from…yeah, we had the whitewashed cottages and village green going on.

I arrived in the US during my third year of university, as an engineering design undergraduate, and I wasn't intending to stay more than six months. As far as the folks back home were concerned, it was the usual fairy tale. English boy goes to America to study, meets the girl of his dreams, all sweet cherry pie and sparkly white, super-straight smile. They get engaged, get married, rent a fabulous apartment in the city, find fabulous high-powered jobs, yada, yada, yada.

It was nothing of the sort.

For a time we considered moving back to England, but that's long since passed. Elise would have needed to retrain in English law, plus…well, I didn't really want to pick up where I left off. Specifically, I didn't want my mother thinking we could just carry on as if the argument never happened. Because that's the kind of woman my mother is. If she doesn't like something, she expects it to change for her—perish the thought that anyone tell her to amend *her* opinions, and she is *very* opinionated. So I delayed telling her, even though I knew all through high school, even though she nearly caught James and me fooling around. It's one of the few bonuses of heterosexism—that parents let same-sex friends enter their child's bedroom sanctuary with no thought to anything untoward taking place.

James and I had quite a few "sleepovers" during the seven wonderful months of our relationship. I use the terms "wonderful" and "relationship" relatively—when you're sixteen and it's your first, it has a certain magic, but it's really not that great. True, my memory likes to play up the romance a little. In my head, James and I hold hands at the movies, cuddle together while we wait for the bus, whisper "I love you." In reality, we mostly ignored each other outside of my single bed, where we'd suck each other off, in the dark, under the covers and as quickly as possible. The night my mother *almost* caught us, she walked straight into the room and flicked on the light. We hoped all she saw was a lumpy mass under the duvet, as we'd heard the door open and stayed deathly still, holding our breath, *praying* she wouldn't pull back the covers. We heard the light switch click again, and I bravely stuck my head out, peering into the gloom, come all over my hands, because her timing was impeccable. I clambered out of bed, went to grab something from the laundry hamper to clean myself. It was missing. So long, sleepovers. So long, James.

University was better though. Away from home at last, I finally got to be myself. No steady relationships during that first year, but there were a few of us who'd hang out together, and pair up on occasion. We were all in the same boat. We'd fumbled our way through adolescence, arriving in higher education with virtually no experience, compared to our straight fellow students. There was only Donny who'd lost his virginity before uni, and he was a total idiot.

"Top or bottom?" he asked me one night, knowing how drunk I was, and also that I didn't have the first clue what he was talking about. When I failed to reply, he elaborated, "Do you like to fuck, or be fucked?"

I don't recall my response to that. Whatever, by next sunrise I'd done both and concluded that I was more of a "top." Donny had evidently forgotten his first time and wasn't exactly gentle. Lucky he only had a small dick, or I'd probably be dead now. *Undergrad impaled on penis*. Way to go! So anyway, that was the Grand Losing Of My Virginity—a night with Donny Dickless and his amazing talking testicles. I kid you not, those boys squeaked and creaked like a pair of old men at a bus stop. Weird.

Second year…

I'm tempted to skip this part, as it was the lousiest year of my life. Long story short, the student exchange worked both ways, and with the influx of "Yanks" came Calvin. Tall, blond, skinny, blue-eyed beauty that he was, if you cut him open you'd find a housebrick where his heart should be. I think, maybe, for me at least, it was love at first sight. He walked into our student accommodation block, and I felt the earth move—not Calvin's doing, but a tremor. We find earthquakes terribly unBritish, and this little guy shook up a mighty magnitude 1.2—kind of average for our side of the Atlantic, but not quite enough to rattle the cups off their saucers (we don't *all* own these, by the way).

I frowned at Calvin. "Did you feel that too?"

"Uh huh," he replied, dropped his holdall in the middle of the floor and wandered off in search of the bathroom, scratching his ass. When he returned, he looked me up and down.

"You're gay," he stated.

It was my turn to go, "Uh huh." No idea why I owned up, just like that. I must have somehow picked up on the subtle vibe being thrown off by his rolled-up sleeves, deck shoes and the dozen LGBT buttons adorning his jacket.

"Cool. Me too," he said.

No shit, Sherlock!

And then he kissed me.

I'm going to cut straight to the end here, because that relationship sucked. I should've realized he was a player. The buttons, the whole "out and proud" routine? Cal was a walking-talking advert for himself. A one-man sex show. Anytime, anyplace, any-fucking-where. And like I said, I thought I was in love right from the get-go. By the time he was returning home to the US, I'd enrolled in the exchange for my third year, not to be near him, but I figured if Cal was getting laid so much…

Oh, I should mention that in the middle of all this he dumped me and I went home for a few weeks. Heartbroken, I came out to my mother. She actually swooned for real.

"Gay, like Freddie Mercury?" she asked, fanning her face with a copy of *The Guardian*. I nodded dumbly. "But he died of that AIDS, Solomon, darling."

That AIDS? Do you mean the bad AIDS, Mother?

I said nothing.

"And Rock Hudson. He died of the AIDS too."

Honest to God.

I said, "That was a long time ago, Mum. And they were famous." As if being famous were a requirement.

She said, "Well, you'll just have to find yourself a girlfriend."

Erm, hello? I'm gay.

"Yes," she continued, making a rapid and complete recovery, "Lizzie was asking after you only the other day. She always liked you."

How stupid of me to not see this coming. The argument that followed was a total farce, with her refusing to accept that I could possibly be gay, and me trying to persuade her that I was by further incriminating myself with confessions of all my first-year adventures, and even that time she came to get the laundry and nearly caught James and me.

"Which time?" says she.

"I…"

"I always assumed you were playing tents."

Always? *Always?* Shit!

"Playing tents? Mum, we were sixteen years old." There was only one sort of "playing tents" we were doing.

So, add to denial this total invasion of privacy, and that pretty much sums up the only conversation we ever had about it.

Back to the student exchange—yeah, OK, I lied. I signed up, among other things, to be near Cal. Luckily (for me, not for him) he'd failed the UK component of his course and got kicked out of college.

Which brings me back to Elise.

She knew I was gay. She'd always known, and so was she, except she was so far back in the closet she had a residency visa for Narnia. She remained the only American woman I knew who didn't call her female acquaintances "girlfriends," because, more often than not, that's exactly what they were. We were fast friends at college, we remained so, and she was a wonderful, beautiful woman. I loved her. She loved me. We did sex OK too, which was how we came up with the marriage of convenience idea. I wanted to stay stateside. She was going to be a successful lawyer. And, God forgive me, I didn't want people to know I'm gay. It all came back to Donny, and Cal.

And James.

Ironically, other than "the beard," my sex life was going the same way as Donny's and Cal's. I'd never asked the question Donny asked of me. Most of the guys who happened to walk my way were happy to be the "passive recipient," though I wished sometimes they would turn the tables. And for all my desperation and frustration, I tried to be gentle, do it properly, get it right. I hoped I was a generous and considerate lover.

As for James—well, you know that quaint little English hometown of ours? With its picturesque village green, fourteenth-century chapel, sheep grazing on hills, watched over by black and white dogs, bare-beam pubs serving real cask ales and steak and kidney pies, church fetes, May Day parades… and knife-wielding lowlife cowards running in packs, playing Hunt the Homo.

Rest in peace, James Coolican. My first, and only, boyfriend. So far…

Chapter Three

Never say never, eh? That's one thing us Brits are famous for—that stiff upper lip of ours. Well, I don't know about upper lips, but Captain Impatient certainly had something going on in the stiffness department, and he'd got my attention.

I was sitting in my office, on the seventh floor of the Magda Building, the view from my window a stunning vista…or not, unless 1970s beige stucco is your thing. Have you ever studied the external wall of a Best Western? I mean *really* studied? I have. Sometimes I wondered if the hotel's windows were actually two-way mirrors installed the wrong way round, or if the people who stayed there had a fetish for being voyeured. The guy in the second room from the end, for instance, had been staying a while, and he'd usually just got out of bed as I arrived at the office, which was a pretty nice way to start the day in my opinion. And the thing was, he'd made eye contact with me across the void a couple of times, so I knew he could see me, yet there he was, standing proud and supremely erect that fine spring morning. A full body stretch, a couple of strokes along the full length of his cock, and then he moved away from the window. A rap at my office door instantly declared a ceasefire on the twitching in my pants.

"Come," I called, suppressing a childish smile at my own inadvertent innuendo. The door opened slowly, and George backed into the room, muttering something in her nervy, girly way at someone outside. I got up and poured two cups of coffee. George closed the door and spun to face me.

"Oh!" she said, surprised to find me right in front of her.

"Morning, George," I greeted, passing her one of the cups.

"Hi there, Sol." She accepted my offering with a gracious nod and took up residence in the chair on the other side of the desk to my own. "How are you this morning?" she asked.

"Fine, thanks. You?"

"I'm great, thank you for asking."

George was my boss, and not at all what you'd imagine. She was in her late fifties, a grandma, widowed young, and the best designer in the firm, no competition. Her full name was Georgette Mary Ann Cooper, of southern stock, from somewhere deep down in Texas, with the drawl to match, and she could shoot out a light from fifty yards, given the right firearm and a finger or two of whisky. Add to this that she was a good foot shorter than I, and deferred to most everyone else, well, she was a walking, talking contradiction.

Talking being the operative word.

There was a call I wanted to make, after all.

Still, I tried to listen intently to her report back on the meeting with the board about our current projects. What did we do? Design office chairs. Exciting, huh? They were George's designs, re-imagined by a team of six. My job was to liaise with the prototype guys, which was pretty cool, as we were in the days of the 3D printer, and it was slow but kind of like magic. Key in the details, press the big green "go" (not quite), and it would eventually spit out a basic solid model, or the simulated multiple parts, depending on the design. Anyway, I won't bore you with all the ins and outs of the job, other than to say that's why George was there that morning, getting between me and my call. Hm, maybe we were compatible after all.

So, she was chattering away, pausing every now and then to take a speedy slurp from her coffee cup, and I really was trying to listen, but my mind kept wandering back to the checkout line the night before, the feeling of him up against my ass, his hand on my shoulder, his scent…

George stopped talking. Staring out the window, she said, "That guy's waving at me and he's butt-naked."

Carefully swiveling in my chair I glanced over, making more of a deal than I needed to of seeking out the window in question. "So he is," I said.

"Isn't that against the law?" George asked. I assumed she meant his nudity rather than his greeting. It likely was, but it wasn't stopping her from taking in the thick fullness of his morning glory. Man, that guy was hung. I dragged my gaze back and studied George's face. I laughed. She blushed. "I think you should go tell the hotel manager," she advised.

"Me?"

"Yeah, you." She folded the drawings back into their protective wallet and got up. "After you've spoken with Merv."

I nodded, and said, "Sure thing, boss," wondering all the while what I was to speak to Merv about. He was the guy who programmed the 3D printer.

I'd have got up to see George to the door, but I was sporting a hard-on like the trunk of a redwood, so I stayed where I was, watching her totter her way across my office. It's not that big a space—big enough for a desk and a couple of chairs, with pacing room—yet it seemed to take her an age to reach the door. She gripped the handle, turned back and gave me one of those smiles that tells you you're about to hear something you won't like from someone who doesn't want to say it, like the friend elected to inform you that your boyfriend's cheating on you.

"It's none of my business," she started tentatively, sighed and changed direction. "Though I guess it is, since it impacts on Magda." She gave me that smile again and shrugged. "Some of our investors wouldn't take too kindly to the company you keep after hours."

"What company's that, George?" I asked, knowing exactly where she was going with this.

"All I'm saying is, you should take advantage of your Magda benefits. The gym in the basement has all the latest equipment."

As I'd thought. See, the gym I belonged to was, in a previous existence, something of a hook-up joint. It remained a gay-friendly establishment, which was, of course, why I joined that particular gym and forked out unnecessary dollars on a monthly basis, when I could've been using the company gym for free.

Halfway out, halfway in, George peered back at me, the smile gone, in its place an expression of regret. "Maybe you could be a little more discreet, is all."

Her parting words. The door closed on the reminder of the other reason why Elise and I had decided to marry. I reclined my chair and studied the strip light running over my desk, aware of the pressure of my phone against my hip, my enthusiasm for making that call all but gone. I got up, grabbed my jacket, and left.

***

Room 702. From the outside I'd counted the windows up and across, so I was almost certain this was the right one. It was hot and I was starting to sweat. I took off my jacket, slung it over my shoulder and approached the door. I knocked twice.

No one home. That was easy. Easy and disappointing.

I turned away, heading back for the elevator. It would have made more sense to just mention it to the girl on reception— "The guy second right on the seventh floor waved hi at my boss this morning…with his dick." Funny as it sounded in my head, I didn't think the kid at the desk would find it quite so amusing. And what if they called the cops? No. It was better to do this in person. I was only trying to protect his dignity. Wasn't I?

I called the elevator, watched the numbers flicker through to seven, a muted ding sounding its arrival. The doors opened. A guy stepped out, passing me by without a second glance. Not him. My delay almost cost me my ride, and I squeezed through the rapidly diminishing gap. Back to ground. Doors open. Ah. This was my guy. He got in. I didn't get out.

"Hey," he said, nodding—with the head on his shoulders for once.

"Hey," I replied. His expression told me he knew who I was. I must have been giving off the same signal. He pressed the button for the seventh floor. I watched him gazing across the small square expanse we were sharing, his eyes fixed on the control panel, a slight smirk on his lips. From my office he'd looked kind of OK. Up close he was more than OK. I'd say he was in his early twenties, and tall and slim, with short brown hair, matching soul patch, long, straight nose and nut-brown eyes. They turned on me now. He was sexy as hell, and we were going up, up, but…

Any other time but this. Any other goddamn time. What the hell was wrong with me?

The elevator stopped, did that *thunk* again. He got out, heading toward 702. I held the doors.

"Listen," I said. He stopped walking and glanced back. The words escaped me. "I, err…"

He looked amused.

"Just, err, wrap up warm, OK?" So lame! "There's snow on the way." I released the doors and watched him walk away.

Chapter Four

I was right about one thing at least. The snowstorm hit as I pumped thirty-five pounds of rubber and iron with my right bicep, watching the sudden flurry swirling past the tiny window set ten feet up in the black wall. I changed arms and continued pumping, no idea how many reps I'd done, my mind not on the job. Story of my day.

The gym was quiet—a couple of guys thumping out a steady rhythm on the treadmills and an older guy chest-pressing on the bench. I don't recall a visit to the gym when he wasn't there somewhere. He was still living in the clone days, a huge handlebar mustache covering the entirety of his top lip, thick black crew-cut hair, both courtesy of Just for Men. He was in good shape and kind of good-looking, if you're into older guys, which I wasn't. I knew that a lot of the gym regulars were into guys a little younger than themselves, me included. Don't get me wrong—they still had to be legal, but I'd come to realize that as we age our tastes don't change, and to my mind the most physically attractive guys tended to be in their early to mid-twenties, which meant my rebuttal of Best Western 702 made even less sense. He was exactly the type I went for—young, anonymous, temporary resident of the city—it couldn't have been more perfect.

See, here's the thing with a marriage of convenience. No two ways about it, I loved Elise, and she loved me. We were both painfully aware of the sacrifices we were making, for our careers, for our families, and we went into it willingly. On our wedding night, she confirmed what she'd said from the beginning. She didn't want to know what I was up to, or who with, so long as it had no bearing on "us." I was OK with that, because even though we lived just outside of Boston, MA, and gay marriage was made legal before we moved there, it didn't mean a thing in my line of work. There might have been more women going into engineering, but it remained a straight industry. Whether it involved the physical work of construction or the office job of design that I did, gay engineers were a rare breed. Or should I say *out* gay engineers. There were no doubt plenty of us, but it was a no-go, and on our wedding night, Elise had used the very same phrase George had used that morning. *Be discreet.*

My attention was snapped back to what I was doing by Tony's blotting out of the light as he passed me by, loaded fifty pounds onto a dumbbell and took up residence on the last vacant bench.

"How you doing, Sol?" he asked. No eye contact. The Velcro fastener of his wrist brace made a satisfying rasping rip as he pulled it free, tugged to tighten it, and stuck it back in place.

"Yeah, not so bad. You?"

"I'm good." Tony flexed and shrugged his hefty shoulders. He was what my dad would call "a big lad"—about six four and an easy three hundred pounds, some of it muscle, some of it not. He was a decent guy, a Canadian, which he took a lot of flak for. And like most of the gym's members, he was out, which was what George had been referring to. My patronage sent the message loud and clear. Funny how it'd taken almost eight years for anyone to notice.

My left arm gave out, and I returned the weights to the rack. I'd been in an hour already, hoping to distract myself from thinking about…him. By that point, I'd realized it was inevitable. I was going to call him sometime. I wasn't really sure why I hadn't already, other than his phone conversation in the store and the implication of the pause and confirmation. Like I said, why should I care if he was in a relationship? My permit was "sex only." It made no difference if he was involved with someone else or not.

Allegedly.

And then there was the rest of it. He wasn't my type. He was my age, if not a little older, the same physique, similar height. Were it not for his coloring being the opposite of mine, we could've been brothers. Now that was a freaking weird thought. No, he looked nothing like me. His hair was almost jet-black, whereas mine is what the folks back home call mousy-brown. It's dead straight and I keep it short and gelled, or it falls in my face. And where he was olive-skinned, I'm very fair. I used to spend a small fortune on sunbeds, until I saw the damage it was doing, like time-lapse footage, no wrinkles one day, the complexion of a seventy-year-old the next. The alternative was the bottled variety, so I settled on my natural skin tones, got used to being a pale Limey. I wouldn't have said I was comfortable in my skin, though—it's a tough claim to make when you're living a lie.

By the time I left the gym that night the snow had stopped, leaving a thin white blanket covering the city. After living there eight years, I should've been used to the Boston weather, but it always felt out of sync. It was March, and back in England the daffodils would be a sea of nodding yellow heads, the nights would be lighter, and warmer. Spring would definitely be on its way. March in Boston, the nights were still freezing, and if it rained, the city would often end up covered in ice that would slowly melt during days that were either a lot warmer than I was used to, or even colder than the east coast of England in winter (and it could get really, bloody cold). I wondered if I'd ever get used to spending half the year sweltering, the other half freezing my ass off. The summer I found stifling—I hated the constant drone of air conditioning, and the humidity was unbearable. I think the seasons arrive a month later in that part of the US than they do in the UK, and while it's still a temperate climate, it's just that little bit more extreme than back home.

Home.

I hadn't thought of it that way in a long time. The truth was, though it pained me to admit it, I was missing it. Not all of it. I was having something of a problem putting my finger on what exactly I was homesick for. Certainly not my parents, and not the small-minded town in which I grew up. I had fun at university, but it was transient, and I'd had no aspirations to study beyond graduation. I wasn't into the club scene, and I was still in touch with my friends online. In short, there was nothing to miss. The culture of Boston, with its curious Irish infusion, wasn't that far removed from the big cities back…in the UK. I enjoyed my job, I liked my life, and I loved my wife.

I was still running down all the possible reasons for the sudden onset of the homesick blues as I returned to an empty apartment and headed for the shower. And that was when it hit me—when I reached out to turn on the tap, uh, I mean faucet. Yep. That was it, right there. Divided by a common language, as they say. Having a conversation could be so exhausting, the constant self-editing, translating on the fly. I *rode* the *elevator* up to our *apartment*. We went to the *store* for *groceries*, and sometimes I forgot my *cell*, left it on the *banquette*. There again, was my yearning for the sounds of home simply a well-concocted excuse for calling that number I'd stored on my *mobile* the previous day?

After my shower, I pulled on a pair of sweats and a tee, grabbed a beer and tried to decide on something to eat. It was past nine, and I couldn't recall Elise saying she was working late. I needed her to be home, to stop me doing something I'd regret. I picked up my phone, tapping it against my teeth. The ball was in my court. All I had to do was call up that number. No big deal. I unlocked the screen, scrolled through my contacts, down to "C"—well what else was I supposed to save his number under? I still had no idea what the guy's real name was. I wasn't sure finding out was the wisest move.

I stared at the screen a long time after it turned dark, trying to find a reason to call, a reason not to, hence my inaction. I got another beer, called out for pizza, and opened my laptop. My phone vibrated. I jumped and checked the screen, disappointed to see Elise's name displayed. Why would it be him? He didn't have my number. I had his.

"Hey, hon," I answered casually.

"Hey. I forgot to say I was going out with Jennifer tonight."

"OK, no problem."

A moment's pause followed. I got the impression Elise expected me to say something else.

After a few seconds more, she said, "There's a steak in the refrigerator."

"I've got pizza on the way," I explained, then, as an afterthought, "What time will you be home?"

"I've had a couple glasses of wine, so I'll stay here. See you tomorrow night?"

"Sure."

Elise hung up. So much for saving my ass. I was out of excuses. I pulled up his number again and hit "call."

Chapter Five

If there's one "Americanism" I really like, it's the one that was most fitting right at that moment.
Son of a bitch.
Twenty-four hours of plucking up the courage to call and I get an out-of-service message. I went to bed, feeling angry, mostly at myself for making such a huge deal out of it. But then it made no sense. I mean, why? Why had he left a fake number in my wallet? What was the point? Unless he was playing games. Yeah, that would be about right. The guy clearly got off on winding people up, pushing into checkout lines, rubbing up against strangers. And there it was again. I was hard. More than that, I was aching for release. All the guys I'd known and not one had got me worked up like that. Sex for one is lonely, but it does the job, which was as well, given that it was the second time that day I found myself jacking off to the fantasy of jamming my cock into his supercilious mouth, laughing as he gagged with my hands on the back of his head, my fingers combing through that thick wavy brown-black hair, the salty scent of him filling my nose, my mouth, oh God, what the fuck…

***

Best Western 702's curtains were closed when I got to my office the next morning, and when they opened it looked like he'd followed my advice about wrapping up warm, more's the pity. I'd blown my chances there. Ha! I wish! To think, the previous morning the toughest decision I had to make was the best of two. Yeah, life sucked right at that moment, or didn't, as the case may be, and George was out for the day, so no discussions or distractions to look forward to. For all of thirty seconds I contemplated heading down to the design workshop, decided I couldn't face it and set up the coffeemaker. It gurgled comfortingly.

Some American dream this was.

While the coffee dripped, I logged on to my computer and called up Jennifer's online profile. She was a paralegal at Kelly and Associates, the firm Elise had started working for three months previously. I'd met Jennifer at the firm's Christmas bash, so I knew what she looked like, and I knew she was bisexual. And single. She'd advertised herself quite freely at that party, making sure everyone was very clear on that. It seemed, therefore, a good idea to find out a little more about her, know my competition, as it were.

See, for as much as Elise knew as well as I did that our marriage was a sham, we were still supposedly making a go of it. Or maybe I was the one making a go of it while she was laughing behind my back. And it was she who'd set the rules. All the sex I wanted, so long as it was of the "no strings" variety. A license for non-stop fun, you might think. Because that's all guys ever think about, right?

Wrong. So wrong.

I wouldn't have classed myself as romantic, though I did love Elise. I loved her very much once, and would have been insane with jealousy if she'd been spending all her time with someone else. Right at that moment? I think I was more annoyed than jealous. Kind of relieved, too.

The coffeemaker stuttered to a stop. I poured a cup and took it over to my window, glancing across to room 702. Not-so-naked guy was doing the same—standing in his window, cup in his hand. He gave me an arms-wide shrug. *Yeah, buddy, I hear ya.* I'd messed up, and I wasn't humble enough to go over there and admit it to him, not even for a lay. I shrugged back and turned away, taking in my gloomy office. No photos on my desk, no executive toys, just a phone and the tools of my trade—notepad, pen, tablet, stylus and computer. I didn't like clutter. It got in the way of clear thinking. Clutter. Like all the shit in my head. I sat down, picked up the pen, absently sketching as I mulled over…nothing. I didn't have time for this. We had four projects in progress, with tight turnarounds, and there I was, doodling like a bored schoolboy.

The phone rang and jolted me out of my misery. I momentarily considered letting it go to voicemail, but picked up. "Sol Brooks," I greeted drearily.

"Mr. Brooks, this is the reception desk."

I waited. When she said nothing further, I prompted, "Yes?"

"There's a gentleman by the name of Mr. Ashton here to see you. He says you're expecting him. Shall I send him up?"

Grant Ashton was my counterpart at ATD Solutions, an industrial interior design firm on the other side of town. To my knowledge none of the projects we were working on was for ATD, but I've been known to be wrong.

"Sure," I said. I hung up and opened the projects folder on my computer, scanning over the documents within. There was nothing close enough to completion to have gone out in a mailshot, which gave rise to another thought. The last time we'd had a problem with one of our products and George had been out of town, it fell to me, as senior engineer, to deal with it. It was sensible to conclude, therefore, that Ashton was here to complain, and in George's absence, I was going to have to carry the can.

A sensible conclusion, but a wrong one. For when I opened the door, who should walk in…drums, please! Captain Impatient!

"Mr. Brooks," he said with a very serious, businesslike nod, though his clothing was casual—deep-blue jeans, and a black leather jacket over a white open-necked shirt. Utterly thrown by his presence, I slammed the door and rounded on him. He offered me a congenial smile and held out his hand—that same hand he had laid on my shoulder two days ago.

"Adam Ashton," he said.

I delayed on the handshake, not intentionally to snub him, simply because I was kind of struggling to catch my breath, never mind shake the guy's hand. I'd been expecting *Grant* Ashton, from ATD. Instead, I'd got *Adam* Ashton. I wasn't complaining. Far from it. As his arm started to drop, I quickly lifted my own and we shook. Like nuclear fusion. I held on with every bit of willpower I possessed, trying to contain the eruption within. I released his hand.

"Coffee?" I offered.

"That'd be great, thanks."

I strode across to the filter, not that it took more than two strides, but I felt it was important to make my mark. This was *my* office.

"What, err…"

"I thought I…"

We both started talking at the same time. I gestured for him to continue.

"It suddenly dawned on me last night, at the gym…"

Did he need to say where he'd been? Of course he did, like I'd needed to stride across my own office.

"…that number I gave you? That's my old phone."

"Right?" I poured the coffee, acting as if it were news to me that the number was a dud.

"I wasn't sure if you'd tried to call."

I nodded once to indicate I'd understood, not to confirm I'd tried to call. "Do you take sugar?"

"No, thanks." He took the cup from me and sipped, letting out one of those little post-sip sighs we all do. "So did you?"

"Huh?"

"Try to call."

"Oh." Straight to the point. That's my Captain Impatient.

My Captain Impatient?

"Yeah," I admitted. "I only got around to it last night, after my workout."

I wondered if that sounded as stupid to him as it did to me. Why were we posturing like this? Actually, that was a little unfair to him. He was on my turf, and it was the third time he'd taken the initiative, so I could understand why he might feel the need to assert a certain level of dominance. And to be equally fair to myself, any hot-blooded male in my position would respond in kind, by which I mean to protect their territory and their position, as opposed to the erection threatening to shove its way through the front of my pants. Adam was perched on the corner of my desk, his legs crossed at the ankle, nursing the coffee cup in one of those big, hot hands of his. He adjusted his position, and I couldn't help but glance down. Yeah, he was having the same problem as me, except he didn't seem to think it was a problem. I looked up again, and he gave me a lopsided smile.

"How long have you been in Boston?" he asked.

"Eight years. Before that I was in Philly for two years. You?"

"Eighteen months. It's a great city."

"Yeah," I agreed. "The weather's fucking awful."

Aw, don't judge me. I'm British, and I was feeling…I don't know. Kind of giddy.

"Tell me about it," he said. He glugged the coffee thoughtfully, his eyes delving deep into mine. He sipped, I sipped, we stared. What the hell was this? A contest? Great. I was high school champion, he didn't stand a chance.

Wrong again.

He disarmed me with another smile. I broke away, somehow made it across the room to my chair, but remained on my feet. Adam set his cup on the desk, pushed off and followed me, stepping into my space. He reached past me, tugged the cord to shut the blinds, his scent enveloping me, knocking my legs from under me, or maybe that was his hand on my chest. I thought he was going to push me down into my chair, and then what? Unzip his pants? Not that I would have minded, but it was a bit fast, even for him.

Instead he said, "There's a man in a window across the street. He's watching you."

I laughed in relief, and embarrassment.

"Ah, yeah," I sighed, like it was a small and unwanted hassle. "At least he isn't naked this time."

"You and he…"

I sensed the tension in his voice.

"No," I confirmed. I felt Adam relax. Wow. That was something. Guess we both had it pretty bad. "I did go to see him yesterday with that in mind, but I went off the idea."

I didn't know why I'd told him that, or how I was talking, or if I was making any sense. Adam's palm was still on my chest, and it should've felt inappropriate, invasive, but it didn't. I put my hand over his, my intention to lift it away, free myself of the grip he had on me, and I did succeed in removing it from my chest, but found I couldn't let go of him. Not even for a second. He rotated his lower arm so that we were palm against palm, brushing his thumb across the back of my hand, both of us watching it happen. I closed my eyes. When I opened them again, I met his intense gaze.

"You OK?" he asked. Those eyes of molten metal were warm with concern.

"Yeah, just…" I didn't have an end to that sentence, other than the truth, which was freaking me out.

"You're married," he observed. I nodded to confirm. "To a guy?"

"No." Maybe he thought Elise was just a friend.

"But you are into guys."

I nodded again.

He glanced over my desk, I guess searching for the usual spousal portrait. He started to laugh, released my hand, and I suddenly felt lost, alone. He moved away, picked up my notepad.

"I'm no psychologist," he said, "but surely a parachute has got to mean something?"

It meant something, all right. I was falling fast. He picked up the pen and scribbled on the pad.

"I'd better go," he said. He took my hand again and gently kissed the back of it, like we were embarking on a courtship of days gone by. I felt the hairs all up my arm stand on end, my skin tingle, a ring of fire in the shape of his soft, warm lips leaving their invisible impression. He released me.

"I need to get to work. That's my current number." He tilted his head in the direction of the pad. "Call me? We can maybe go for a drink later."

He finished the rest of his coffee, dumped his empty cup on my desk and left. When I finally recovered, I opened the blinds and saw Best Western 702 step away from his window. I hoped I was backing the right horse.

Chapter Six

There was no doubt in my mind that Adam was interested, which should have made the decision to call him an easy one. Still I delayed. The thing was, I could see we were already way past being just a one-off, beyond even being a meaningless fling. For the first time since Elise and I got together, I was facing the prospect of a relationship, because no one as good-looking and impatient as Adam went to those lengths to secure a one-night stand. Or maybe he just liked the thrill of the chase. Whichever, I was dancing through a mine field that could blow Elise's and my marriage to smithereens, taking the rest of our carefully constructed lives with it.

And a big part of me thought, *What the hell!* In all honesty, right at that moment the prospect of spending just a couple of hours with him was worth risking everything. It was terrifying and exhilarating all at once. I wanted him more than I had ever wanted anything or anyone, including Calvin, and maybe even James.

To cover my tracks, I went for a quick workout on my way home, meaning I could claim that the shower and shave were for that reason. However, it was Thursday—a night I rarely went to the gym, for historical reasons. In the past it had been my night out with the guys, so why was I being so cagey? After all, wasn't I going for a night out with the guys?

OK, *a* guy.

I got home to find a pink Post-It stuck to the fridge.

> *Catching a movie with the girls.*
>
> *See you at 11. x*

Well, that kind of made things easier for now, though I couldn't help but wonder which girls Elise meant, and whether singular might be more accurate in her case also.

I showered quickly but shaved slowly and dowsed myself in my best cologne. I probably left most of it on the dozen or so shirts I put on and took off again, before finally settling on one I wanted to wear. The truth kind of hit me then. I had a date with Adam. I tried to ignore the sensation of my heart fluttering in my chest, locked up the apartment and headed out into the chilly evening.

We were meeting at a bar near Emerson, which suited me fine, as it was a train ride away, so the chances of bumping into anyone I knew were slim. I took the T to Boylston Street and walked to the bar in question, surprised to find that it wasn't a gay bar, perhaps somewhat less surprised to find my date had yet to arrive. I ordered a Bud and opted for sitting at the counter. The place was quiet, a few students huddled in dark corners, ghastly white faces illuminated by cell phones. Speaking of which, there was mine now.

"Hello?" I answered, trying not to sound disappointed.

"Hey, sorry."

Didn't I know this was coming?

"I'm running late."

"OK." I was seriously hacked off, but I kept my voice flat. "You want to cancel?"

"Not at all. Something came up, but I'll get there soon as."

He rang off.

Were it not for the fact that I'd just traipsed halfway across the city to meet him, I'd have walked right out of there and got straight back on the train home. OK, slight over-exaggeration. It was a twenty-minute journey, tops, but I was torn between avoiding the humiliation of being stood up, and an embarrassingly desperate requirement to see him again. Was there a pattern emerging? Pisses me off, turns me on. Could I honestly live like that? I was wound tight as a spring.

I wanted to see Adam so much it was almost a need. I drank my beer, ordered another. Half an hour passed. I considered heading off to see if Best Western 702 was still checked in. Hell, I was so horny I could probably have made room for big Tony at the gym. Yeah, horny. And lonely. I downed my second beer, ordered a third.

I was on my fifth when Adam finally showed his face. I'd been through annoyed, impatient, worried, morose—now I was back to plain old angry, with some very interesting ideas on how to get it out of my system.

"Hey." His tone was apologetic. He mimed drinking from a bottle by way of asking if I wanted another. I shrugged my consent. Why not? I wasn't going anywhere, not now. I watched him order our beers. He was wearing snug-fitting black jeans over black boots, a gray wool shirt and white tee. And he was freshly showered. His cologne wafted my way—a mix of sandalwood and musk. It might have been his own musk.

He passed me a beer, his fingers deliberately brushing against my hand in the process. I tried to cover the startling effect it had on me with a dismissive raise of the eyebrows.

"You're lucky," I said. "I was about to give up on you."

"I appreciate you waiting. You don't strike me as the patient type."

Excuse me? This from the guy who couldn't wait his turn at the checkout?

"I presume there's a good reason you left me standing around for an hour?" I sounded indignant, and childish. He didn't seem to notice.

"A reason, yeah. Not a good one." He glanced around the bar room. It was getting busy. "Have you eaten?"

I shook my head. I wasn't hungry, which I put down to the beer. Gassy beer, nothing more.

"There's a steakhouse not far from here. What do you think?"

"Sure," I agreed. I could use a little more protein in my diet, and a lot more Adam in my evening.

We finished our beers in silence. He obviously had something on his mind. He was frowning and that increasingly familiar smirk was absent. When we left the bar, I decided to do the decent thing.

"You wanna talk about it?" I asked.

"No, but I think I need to." He was still frowning, his hands in his pockets, eyes trained on the pavement a few steps ahead of us. "We just found one of the college kids dead."

"Whoa." Now I understood what he meant about it not being a good reason. "What happened?"

"Not sure, but it looks like suicide. It wasn't even my rotation tonight. I just happened to be passing…" He shook his head. "Anyway, I stayed with his roommate until the police and ambulance crew were done. We moved him to a different dorm."

"Look, if you want to give tonight a miss—"

"No, it's fine. I need the distraction." He gave me a watery smile and looked away again. We walked on in silence. I tried to think of something to talk about.

"So you work there?" I asked. *Well that wasn't much of a distraction, was it? Idiot.*

"At Emerson? Yeah, I do."

"Security?" I guessed.

"No. I teach in the Arts faculty. Performing Arts, to be exact."

"You're an art teacher?" I was genuinely surprised.

"Not as macho as engineering, huh?" he said, a little of that spark coming back to his eyes as he glanced my way.

We reached the steakhouse, continuing our conversation while we waited to be seated.

"You know I'm a design engineer, right?"

"Yeah. I figured as much, from your…equipment."

"The stylus and tablet?"

There was that smile again, and just like that my world stopped spinning. The waiter gave it a jump start, showed us to a table, and Adam gestured for me to lead the way, which was very gentlemanly of him. I tried not to get riled by that, or by the hand on my hip gently guiding me forward. Admittedly, that part didn't irritate me quite so much. It already felt right, kind of like we'd been doing it forever, yet not, as it still felt new. The waiter led us to a table at the back of the restaurant and took our drinks order. Adam opted for a beer; I went with a mineral water—too much alcohol and fizz already. I was feeling very relaxed, and a little bit intoxicated.

The restaurant was intimate, with subdued lighting and quiet background music, the tables set a sensible distance apart—cozy, but not crowded. The waiter returned with our drinks and we ordered food. Adam chose New York sirloin, medium rare; I was tempted to do the same, but settled on the rib-eye, also medium rare.

After the waiter had gone, we sat in silence. I had questions I needed to ask, in particular how Adam found out where I worked. I also wanted to know more about his job, how old he was, whether he was single, planning to return to the UK anytime soon—in other words I wanted to know everything about him.

"Tell me…" I began.

"Where…"

We did it again, started speaking at the same time. On this occasion, he let me go first.

"My work address?"

"Your ID card."

I kept my ID card in a concealed pocket behind the dollar bills, my driver's license in the front.

"You went through my wallet?"

Ah, that crooked smile, melting me in an instant. I picked up my glass and sipped steadily. He folded his arms, leaning toward me.

"Bite me," he said.

I choked on my mineral water. That just made him laugh. After a minute or so of me coughing my guts up, I finally regained control, then nearly lost it again when he reached across the table and slid his hand under mine. I did a quick scan of the vicinity. His head tilted in curiosity.

"You're not out?"

"Err, kind of, kind of not."

"Why's that? Work?"

"Mostly. And family, and Elise's work." And a stupid promise I made myself long, long ago.

"Elise is your wife?"

I nodded. "The woman I was with at the store."

"You were with someone?"

"Yeah."

He looked bamboozled. I laughed.

"She's just made junior partner at Kelly and Associates."

"Wow! That's impressive." He examined me for a moment. "I'm guessing you're what? Thirty?"

"Coming up to thirty-one. How about you?"

"Thirty-two next birthday." He retracted his hand. I missed the contact immediately, and was grateful it was only a temporary withdrawal. He removed the wool shirt, hooked it over the back of the chair, sat down and took my hand again.

"Is this OK?" he asked. I nodded and smiled.

It was a million times better than OK. I'd never felt so comfortable in someone else's company, like we were on exactly the same wavelength. I could tell he had as many questions to ask me as I had to ask him, but neither of us was in any rush. How was that even possible, three days after we bumped into each other, and not in ideal circumstances by any stretch?

"In the store," he said edgily. I must have looked puzzled, because he added, "On Monday?"

"Yeah. I knew when you meant. I was just thinking about it too."

"I wanted to explain." His eyes crinkled with embarrassment. "Apologize and explain. I don't generally accost people in supermarkets."

"You tried to push in."

"And you blocked me with your arse."

I loved that he'd said "arse" instead of "ass," but no way was I letting up yet.

"Like I said, you tried to push in."

"That wasn't why I wanted to apologize, but if it bothers you that much, I'm sorry."

"Say it."

He shrugged and laughed in disbelief. "I'm sorry I tried to push in. Better?"

"Yeah." I attempted some more of the mineral water. Our steaks arrived, and he had to release my hand for the plates to be set down. The waiter checked we had everything we needed. I know I did. We both shuffled our chairs a little further under the table, soon discovering there wasn't enough legroom for two six-feet-plus guys. With much knee bumping, we negotiated a space-sharing strategy that involved sitting slightly to the side, our legs interlocked so that we each had one of our knees between the other's. The contact sent an electric pulse racing right through me. I shifted on my chair in an attempt to subtly adjust for the sudden expansion in my pants, saw Adam do the same, and we both started to giggle at how ridiculous this was.

The giggling continued intermittently for the duration of the meal, triggered first by my asking Adam if he was single at the same time as he'd shoveled a significant chunk of steak into his mouth. He put his fork down and chewed frantically, making *mm mm* noises and gesturing with his hand to indicate he would answer just as soon as he could. It seemed to take an age, and all the while I was watching him I giggled like a drunken teenager. To be honest, I felt like a drunken teenager. Finally, he swallowed hard and swigged some beer to wash it down.

"What was the question?" he asked seriously. I shook my head dolefully, and we were both off again. He waited until we'd settled back to our meals before he answered me with a simple, "No."

Ah, shit.

I'd be lying if I said that wasn't the answer I was hoping for. It was a devastating blow to find out he was taken, which was ridiculous. It was no different to me being married. In fact, him being in a relationship was safer all round. Safer, but not enough. I focused on sawing at my tender steak and crammed some in my mouth so I didn't say something I'd regret later.

"Or, at least, I was until tonight."

I put down my fork and examined him. "You're pretty damn sure of yourself."

He nodded. "I'm pretty damn sure how I feel about you."

I had nothing to say to that.

"Face it. I'm the love of your life."

"I'm married."

"To a woman."

"And?"

"You've got a lavender marriage."

"Oh, how quaint!"

"If it's not for show then why are you here?"

That was a good question. Most of the guys I'd hooked up with didn't ask—probably didn't care, and why would they? Sex only. No strings. That's what I kept telling myself. Adam was watching me, and smirking.

"Are you telling me you're in love with your wife?"

"I'm not telling you anything. We don't even know each other."

He nodded, loaded another too-big piece of steak into that luscious mouth of his. "True," he munched. He swallowed thoughtfully and looked me directly in the eye. "But it feels like we do, or is that just me?"

I smiled. "No. It's not just you." A muscle in my leg twitched. That sometimes happens after I've been hitting the leg press too hard. Adam felt the sharp jerk of my knee between his thighs and gave me a questioning look.

"Sorry. Post-workout thing."

He reached under the table and massaged my lower thigh in exactly the right place, instantly easing the cramp. I sighed. He chuckled at me. He was nearly done with his steak. I glanced at my plate to find I was too, which was crazy. I couldn't recall eating any more than a couple of mouthfuls. I crunched my way through a few hand-cut fries and cleared my palate with some water.

"You're right, by the way. About Elise and me."

"Hey, you don't need to tell me anything."

"I want to." I wanted to tell him *everything*. For now, I stuck to the more salient aspects. "Long story short, it suited us both. I wanted to stay in the US, and getting married was the easiest means to achieve that. Elise needed someone who wasn't going to get in the way of her career. She's gay too, not that she's ever said as much."

"Do you screw each other?"

I waited in anticipation of feeling affronted by the bluntness of his question. Strangely I wasn't. "Yeah."

"So you're bi?"

"Nope. I've got a very creative imagination." I grinned. He laughed in response.

"You know, if you ever want to tell me the long version…"

"Let's get to know each other a little first."

"OK. You're on."

"But anyway," I said, deflecting as I realized how little he'd told me so far of his life before we met.

Oh.

I didn't want to think about that too hard. *Before we met*—way too "start of an epoch" when we'd only shared a single dinner date.

"Anyway?"

I'd forgotten he was still waiting for the question.

"Uh, sorry. I lost traction for a second. I was gonna say I've been doing all the talking. What about you?"

"The personal stuff?"

I nodded.

"There's not much to tell. The usual string of guys, some more serious than others. My last ex is the closest I've come to settling down long-term. He's got a PhD in something to do with statistics and works at city hall. He asked me to marry him. I said no."

That must've been tough on them both. I didn't say as much out loud, but Adam seemed to pick up on what I was thinking.

"Water under the bridge. We're all good now."

I wanted to ask why he'd turned down the proposal. Was it because he didn't feel the same way? Or because he wasn't ready to make a commitment? The waiter came to collect our plates. After he left, Adam leaned closer, prompting me to do the same.

"He's with my ex now," he explained.

I followed the direction of his gaze, to the guy working the bar. He couldn't have been much over twenty-one, and he was quite beautiful—thick black hair and emerald eyes. Very Irish. Adam sat back again.

"Not that he's any more the committing type than I am."

That answered my question succinctly. *Again with the disappointment?*

"Did you want to stay for dessert?" Adam asked.

Quick as a flash I came back with, "Depends on the alternative."

I felt myself blushing, surprised at my forthrightness. Adam's eyebrow went up a little, followed by one corner of his mouth. I shook my head and laughed at myself. He waved down the waiter for the check.

The wind had dropped, and it felt a little warmer as we walked the short distance from the restaurant to Adam's apartment. Or maybe it was because he was holding my hand again, his fingers firmly cross-hatched with mine. We must've looked a bit peculiar—two big, built guys, hand in hand, strolling casually, laughing and chatting about all kinds of crazy things. It had occurred to me more than once during the past couple of hours that this was the first time I'd laughed properly in years. Not to mention the attacks of the giggles. It wasn't a behavior I was prone to, not since James. That realization hurt. Really hurt.

I pushed the pain away and continued listening to Adam's stories about the different places we passed by. The mix and mingle of college facilities and other businesses reminded me of Manchester's university quarter, not that I'd been back there recently—*perhaps best not to dwell on that either*, I thought, focusing once again on Adam's commentary. It would have bored me senseless, but for that deep, chocolaty quality to his voice, so sensual yet soothing, never mind his amazing accent—I was interested to know where he'd lived before London, and assumed it was Australia, but I didn't want to interrupt him by asking. I didn't want him to stop talking. Ever.

When we arrived at his apartment, he took out his key, but didn't unlock the door. He watched me for a moment.

"What?" I asked.

"You were a bit quiet for a while back there. Having second thoughts?"

"No." I laughed to cover how vulnerable I felt. "I was thinking about someone from a long time ago."

"Just say if we're going too fast, OK?"

Captain not-so-Impatient after all?

Yeah, right. He didn't even make it as far as the light switch.

Chapter Seven

I wanted to see him, watch his face as his mouth met mine, stare into those liquid eyes as he moved in on me in the unlit hallway. All my other senses were working overtime. The sweet beery taste of his breath filled my mouth, the rough velvet of his tongue pushed hard against mine, his hot hands skimmed my shoulders, brushed down my back, drawing me closer in a suffocatingly tight embrace. He took his time, exploring my mouth, my lips, my neck, and I let him take charge, aware that the increase in my heart rate was only partly due to sexual arousal. I was kind of panicked, by everything—the dark, the overwhelming scent of his body, his confidence, the fact that I wasn't the one controlling the action, that this didn't feel casual. If I allowed this to continue, if I let him in…

"The bedroom's through here," he said, leading me by the hand. A door opened on a room illuminated by moon and street light, a silken drape of silver and gold across the wooden floor and the king-size bed. My heart was beating a tattoo on the inside of my rib cage. It was too dark. *Too dark?* I'd never been afraid of the dark, so why was I being such a wuss?

"Would you mind if we turned on the light?" I asked.

Adam's silhouette passed in front of me, drifting through the platinum gloom, merging with the shadows, and then there was light. Blinding, eye-burningly bright light, and not at all comforting. I must have looked as spooked as I felt, as the next thing I knew, Adam was sitting next to me on the end of the bed, his arm around my shoulders. This wasn't me. This was some crazy imposter taking over my body. Maybe my drinks had been spiked. Maybe he'd spiked them. That'd be right, wouldn't it?

"Look, Sol, if you don't want to do this…"

"No. I do. It's just…" I didn't know what it was. I took a couple of deep breaths, trying to steady myself.

"Has anything bad ever happened to you?"

I turned sharply and stared at him. "Like what?"

He was struggling to find a way to word it.

"I've never been assaulted, if that's what you mean."

"OK." He was noticeably relieved. "I was just thinking about the store the other day, and how if you'd…what I mean is it was embarrassing enough without…added complications."

I watched those mercury pools cloud with guilt. "Hey," I said, taking hold of his hand. "Don't sweat it."

He laughed gently. "I'm gonna make us a coffee."

Good idea. I followed him through to the kitchen, getting my first proper view of his apartment. It was sparsely furnished, tasteful, very masculine. After living with a woman for eight years, I felt qualified to make that judgment. Women fill homes with things of great emotional significance and no practical value, like stuffed toys and ornaments. OK, maybe not just women—some of the guys I'd hooked up with had their fair share of crap lying around the place—but it's not my thing and it clearly wasn't Adam's either. Across the hall I could make out the profile of a large pale sofa, huge TV and fully stacked bookshelves. A dark square covering most of the floor was suggestive of a rug, but otherwise the room was bare. From what I'd seen of his bedroom, not that I'd been paying much attention, it contained little more than his bed.

His kitchen had the usual compliment of electrical appliances, with everything else concealed inside glass-fronted cabinets. I leaned against one and watched him spoon instant coffee into two mugs: matching plain white with black rims. See? Functional. No flowers.

Mugs prepared, he advanced on me slowly, no doubt worried he'd provoke another overreaction. I put my arms around him and smiled apologetically.

"Sorry about before."

"It's fine. Like I said, if we're going too fast…"

"It's not that. I want you, big time, but this? It's…" I lowered my eyes. He leaned in and kissed me gently on the lips.

"Intense?" he offered.

"Yeah."

I probably had a lot more to say, but I forgot the moment his mouth opened against mine. I waited for him to lead. He didn't. I cautiously tested him with my tongue. He allowed me in. His chin rasped against mine, the roughness contrasting exquisitely with the softness of his lips. I ran my hands up and down his back, and he writhed against me. I grabbed his T-shirt, tugged at it to free it from his jeans. He shrugged out of his shirt, flexing toward me so I could pull the stretchy white fabric over his shoulders and head. It's quite a challenge, undressing each other when you're more or less the same height and wearing fitted clothes, but now he stood before me, topless and glorious, his nipples like buttons of dark chocolate topping firm pectoral muscles, well-defined abs, a trail of dark hair running up the center of his lightly sculpted six pack and spreading like the fronds of a palm tree across his olive chest. Good God, he was a fucking magnificent sight. I shifted my gaze, staring into his eyes, willing him to undress me. I wanted to feel his skin against mine, but my earlier resistance made him hesitate.

"Do it," I said. His mouth twitched, fighting the urge to smile. He obeyed, grabbing my shirt and using it to pull me to him, kissing me deeply as he slowly unfastened each button and eased the linen over my shoulders. I was too hot and bothered for it to fall through gravity alone, and he helped it along, our torsos making that first, mind- and body-blowing contact. Like his hands, his chest was much hotter than mine, and the heat radiated through me, front to back, up into my cheeks, down through my groin, as if he'd pumped me full of liquid fire. In a far distant corner of the universe, a kettle came to a boil.

I was wearing my button-fly 501s—evidently my subconscious had been intent on playing hard-to-get all along. The rest of me was just hard, none of it making for an easy mission. Adam puffed and panted, fighting to gain access, his brow squeezed tight in concentration.

"Fuck, Sol. It's like a bloody chastity belt."

I laughed and made to help, but he pushed my hands away.

"I've got it," he insisted.

Aye, aye, Cap'n Impatient. Give him his due, he persevered for a good ten seconds before he raised his arms in surrender. With ease, I peeled the three buttons from their holes and shrugged.

"What was…" I started to say. The rest of it was something about all that fuss, but I'd lost the power of speech again, with his hand inside my jeans, inside my *boxers*. I loved this license to think in my own language, not that there was much in the way of thinking going on, with one hot hand snugly cupping my balls, the other around my dick, the firm yet gentle circle of his finger and thumb easing my foreskin down. He took a breath and frowned, like he was preparing to ask a question but decided against it, and descended to his knees, taking my jeans with him. His hand returned to my balls, his fingers extending behind, stroking right the way back to my hole, and forward again. The sensation was so overwhelming that I almost missed his mouth closing around me, and he went straight for the kill, deep-throating me, no gagging. I thought fleetingly to my recurring fantasy of the past few days. It had served me well, but the reality? Pun intended, it blew me away. Adam really knew what he was doing. More than that, it was as if he knew me. He eased his lips up to the tip again and probed at my slit, glancing up to show off the string of precum connecting his tongue to me. I let out an involuntary groan, put my hand on his head, guiding him down so that his hot, wet mouth enveloped me again.

The thing about being a so-called "top" is that you receive more than your fair share of blow jobs, but rarely get to give them. In that pale imitation fantasy of mine, I'd had him suck me off so I could dominate him. If there'd been time to elaborate, I may well have imagined us fighting in an effort to maintain our position. Not so. As I tried to pull away, he moved with me, sucking me so hard that I was somewhere between yelling in pain and exploding in his mouth.

It turned out he was more patient than I'd thought, as at the next shuddering thrust of my hips, he released me and rose to his feet again, sharing his first taste of me. I had to flex away from him to break contact. I was teetering on the edge, and what a view it was. Time to try a return to the bedroom, where we could continue more comfortably, now I was in the swing of it and no longer freaking out like a teenage virgin. Actually, I guess that was a significant part of my initial reluctance. Adam was making all the moves, and I was expecting that he'd want to fuck me sometime soon. I wanted it too, but the last time was…Donny Dickless. By comparison, Adam was toting the Eiffel Tower. It was going to hurt like hell, and I wasn't sure I could tell him. That, for all of my experience, and I'm honestly not bragging when I say I'd had more than my fair share, if he fucked me, and that was a BIG if, it would only be my second time.

For now, I settled on giving back in kind, pushing him down onto the bed and removing his jeans and shorts. Propped on one arm, he lay on his side diagonally across the plain burgundy duvet, smiling up at me expectantly. The street light's amber reflected off those steely irises of his, heightening the molten metal effect, almost as if his gaze were being recast right in front of me. I knelt on the edge of the bed, and he made a grab for me, attempting to capture me with his mouth. I'd gone soft again and was feeling a little inadequate.

"No." I pushed his face away. He stuck out his bottom lip and looked sad. "Your turn," I said. He rolled onto his back with his hands behind his head. I paused, thrown slightly by his immediate submission. He narrowed his eyes at me.

"I expected you to put up more of a fight," I explained.

He shrugged, as much as it's possible to shrug while lying on your back, and said, "I figured we'd save the fighting for next time." He lifted his ass off the bed, his dick waving at me. That was all the encouragement I needed. Taking my time, I brought my lips down to greet that satiny head with a kiss. He stayed absolutely still, his lilting eyes settling momentarily on my mouth closing around him, then shifting to my rapidly rising erection. His musky scent smelled so damned incredible it was threatening to take me over. I wanted him so much, and yet I sort of didn't know what to do with him. It was the strangest sensation, to be overcome by need and not have the faintest idea how to satiate it. If he'd noticed my confusion he certainly didn't show it, as he was harder than ever, his balls tight against my tongue and lips. I nibbled the base of his dick and slowly worked my way up, licking every part of him, capturing him between my lips. I sucked. He fucked my mouth, his eyes now closed as he pushed down on my head, forcing me to take his full length, my nose buried in his neatly trimmed triangle of coarse, dark hair. A small tattoo peeked over the growth—a tiny green-eyed black cat, prowling on tiptoes along the hairline, tail held high.

He lifted his head to see why I'd stopped. I released him so I could explain, working him with my hand.

"Your tattoo."

"Ah. My uni roommate's doing."

"Drunken misadventure?"

"No. She insisted I needed some pussy."

I chuckled, got set to return to my previous activity. He rolled onto his side and gripped my leg.

"Come here," he said huskily. I allowed him to move me where he wanted me. A sixty-nine. Now that really would have been a first.

Except I couldn't do it.

Maybe I'd been drunker than I'd realized, and I was sobering up, because all of a sudden I needed to escape, get out of there, get away from him. The question was how to do so without losing face. I resisted. He tightened his grip on my leg. I jerked sharply away and staggered to the kitchen to retrieve the abandoned heap of rags that was my clothes. I felt wretched.

"Sol?" Adam appeared in the hallway, watching in bewilderment as I quickly redressed. "Sol, what's wrong?"

"Got a breakfast meeting," I said quickly, which was true, incidentally, but I could've caught the first morning train home and still been at the office in plenty of time. Adam continued to watch me, scratching his head in confusion, stark naked. It would've been funny if I hadn't been in such a state. It was madness. I knew that, but I couldn't help it, and I was shaking so much that I ended up jettisoning my socks to hasten my getaway. As I stumbled past, Adam put his hand on my arm, stopping me in my tracks. I couldn't look at him. I felt such a fool. He was no longer aroused—not surprising—and leaned toward me, kissing me lightly on the cheek.

"Call me. OK?" he said. I nodded, hoping he could tell from my face how bad I felt, how sorry I was. I left.

Chapter Eight

I didn't sleep.
Across the other side of our bed, Elise snored gently, her back turned against me, legs curled up, a foot stuck out of the covers. It was familiar, safe. Depressing. I rolled onto my back, hazily following the flicker across the ceiling, the headlights of scant nighttime traffic, while I tried to comprehend my behavior of a few hours ago. I'd overreacted, but to what? And why? The thoughts whirled around my brain without resolution. I turned onto my left side, closed my eyes. His face appeared on the insides of my eyelids. I lay on my front, started to drift, and was rudely jolted awake by the sensation of falling. One final attempt on my right side—a half hour later I was watching headlights again. I felt sick, and so tired. My teeth hurt, my head was fuzzy, my stomach kept lurching. Flu? If only! I glanced at the clock—a little after six—and gave up.

Solitude in the shower did nothing for me. Miserably, I washed myself, barely a twitch as I recalled being with Adam the night before. Had I not seen enough proof that he was far more patient than I'd given him credit for? Or did I think that all his checking we weren't moving too fast was a ruse to get me into bed? In the past that would've been quite a turn-on, that someone would take such care to seduce me. Instead, all I felt was sadness, that I'd screwed up, that I'd had to walk away. What a fucking idiot I was. Anyone in their right mind would've at least stuck around for the orgasm, but not me. Oh no. I'd felt that tug of something far beyond lust and knew I had to do the decent thing, for him, for me.

So which one of us was impatient?

By the time Elise made it to the kitchen, I was on my third coffee, pretending to read the news on my iPad. She poured herself a cup and sat opposite.

"What time did you get home?" she asked.

"About two."

"Did you have fun?"

"It was OK, yeah."

She sipped her coffee, observing me. I kept my eyes on the screen. My pulse was booming in my ears.

"What's the matter?" she asked. I chanced a quick glance up. She gazed steadily back at me. I shrugged.

"Nothing," I said. Even I could hear how unconvincing it sounded. Elise nodded once. For a split second, her eyes blazed, and then she faked a smile. She let it go. For now.

"You haven't forgotten about picking Mom and Dad up, have you?"

Ah, hell.

"No," I lied. "What time do they land?"

"Five fifteen. They're staying at the same hotel as last time. You know which one?"

I nodded an affirmation. I knew which one. It was the five star behind the Best Western where my once-naked admirer was staying.

"Good," Elise said. "Can you tell Mom I'll get there as soon as I can?"

"Sure."

Elise slid off her stool, put her cup in the dishwasher, kissed me on the cheek and left for work. I followed five minutes later.

***

Breakfast meeting cancelled, one of the projects had fallen through, lunch with the board, trying to justify our request for a budget increase, and an hour-long argument over the color of the prototype with a prospective client who couldn't grasp the concept that it was just that. A prototype, not the final product, asshole. Was it any wonder that by three o'clock I was physically, mentally, and emotionally done in? Were it not for my in-laws flying up for a weekend visit, I'd have left work early and gone for a good, long run. There was nothing like pounding my way through the streets and parks when I felt like…whatever it was I felt like. They were unfamiliar emotions to me, distracting, destructive, hopeless. I could only recall feeling like that once before—when I found out James was dead.

I was at university, and came home for the funeral. His family thanked me for being a good friend, surprised to see me there, as they didn't know about us. They knew about James—everyone knew about James—that was why we were watching his broken body being lowered into a hole in the ground. But whenever I visited I played it absolutely straight, and being there that day I felt relieved and ashamed all at once.

Adam hadn't called. I don't know why I was hoping he would—he was waiting for me to call, and how could I? I'd fled his apartment just as we reached the best bit. No explanation. Not even a goodbye. If I wanted to make absolutely certain he was out of my life for good, all I needed to do was leave it alone. Instead, I pulled my phone from my pocket, scrolled through to "C" in my contacts, running my thumb across the letters, contemplating. I shook my head, an instruction to myself not to do this, tossed my phone onto the desk and buried my face in my hands. A knock at the door. George's faint little *tap-tap-tap-tap*, like the smallest, meekest woodpecker in the world.

"Come," I called. The door opened. George came into view, facing forward for once. She was smiling. Some good news. Thank Christ!

"Sol, how are ya?" she asked, still beaming at me.

"Fine," I answered suspiciously, as we'd only done lunch an hour ago. What did she know that I didn't?

"Excellent," she said. She continued grinning and nodding. She looked slightly insane.

"Care to share?" I asked. I didn't mean to sound terse, but I really wasn't in the mood. Her smile faded, and I was immediately repentant. Too late. Her nostrils flared, her lips thinned to an underscore. She glowered at me, likely weighing up if I deserved letting back in the loop.

"The board just approved your promotion," she said tightly.

"Promotion?" News to me. "Remind me again."

"The second design team."

"But we lost the contract." Our team could handle a maximum of three contracts at a time. The fourth was where the idea for a second team stemmed from: now we were back to three, there was no reason to expand. My phone vibrated across my desk. I straightened up so I could read the screen and felt the blood rush to my cheeks. George glanced at the phone.

"You need to get that?"

"I'll call them back."

She nodded.

"So, this second design team. When did you hear it was still going ahead?"

"We just talked about it over lunch." She looked perplexed. I imagine she wasn't the only one. "Are you coming down with something?"

"No. I'm fine, kinda. Elise's parents are visiting for the weekend."

"Oh."

I knew that would win me some sympathy. They were OK really, in small doses, preferably with us in Boston and them in New York. George was heading for the door.

"You need to confirm your acceptance with the board before you leave this evening," she said.

"Do I have to accept?"

"What the heck are you talking about? It's a promotion, Sol. A fifteen-thousand-dollar raise."

"Yeah, but…" I rubbed the inner corners of my eyes with my finger and thumb. I was getting a headache. "OK." Whatever. I knew the job—it was what I did when George was out of town, except I'd be doing it every day. I was sure I'd feel more enthusiastic once I'd got past the weekend.

When George had gone, I unlocked my phone, staring at the missed call notification. Strike four. I called back. Voicemail.

"Hey. It's Sol. Just returning your call, and…" I swallowed hard. My pride stuck in my throat. "That's all. Catch you later."

I hung up.

***

The drive to the airport gave me time to put my thoughts in order, and it was starting to make some kind of sense. Maybe sense wasn't quite the right word, because two things about the previous night were completely at odds with each other, specifically, Adam's comment about not being the kind of guy to settle down, and then everything else about the way we just clicked. I had no intention of giving up my career and marriage for someone who didn't want commitment. I had no intention of giving up my career and marriage, period. But until he'd said what he did, I'd been hovering in a limbo where for the first time I was wondering, "What if?" In his presence I was completely ensnared, willing to consider the possibilities. Away from him I could rationalize, resist. I needed to make sure we never saw each other again, but I still owed him an apology.

At the airport I parked at Arrivals and waited, watching the information board. At least having Elise's parents around would give me plenty else to occupy my mind. They came through the gate, my mother-in-law scanning the group of us waiting for our respective friends and relatives. Spotting me, she waved and hooked her arm through her husband's, leading him over. He was losing his sight to glaucoma and wasn't far off being completely blind.

"Solomon! How lovely to see you. You look wonderful, dear." Elise's mom tilted her cheek in my direction. Dutifully I kissed it.

"Hey, Darla. You're looking great yourself. Tom?"

"Sol," Elise's dad responded to my greeting. They had carry-on luggage only. I took their bags from them, led the way to the car, and loaded up the trunk while Darla assisted Tom into the front seat. As I opened the driver's side door, I noticed my phone, still on the dash, screen illuminated.

"Captain Patient calling," Darla read off the screen.

Yeah. I'd changed his name. It was the least I could do, and maybe it was just a little wishful thinking, not that it mattered. Once I'd apologized, I was going to delete his number. I dismissed the call and removed my phone from the mount.

"Won't be a second," I explained, stepping out of the car and closing the door. I called him back. He answered right away.

"Hey."

"Hey," I replied, keeping my voice low. "Look, I can't talk now, but I need to say I'm sorry."

"Accepted."

I waited for more. I needed more.

"Was there something else?" he asked.

You, me, the world…

"I owe you an explanation," I said.

"OK. So…you want to meet up?"

"I don't think—" I closed my eyes, willing myself to say it. *I don't think it's a good idea.* "Elise's parents are here for the weekend," was what came out of my mouth.

"Monday then?"

I breathed out heavily. He heard me.

"Sol. If you don't want this, just tell me now."

"I…"

Oh God, how I wanted it. I wanted him.

"Monday," I repeated.

"You coming up to Emerson again, or—"

"No. Meet me at my office."

"OK."

"I've got to go. Bye." I hung up quickly, gave my pulse a minute to return to normal and got back in the car.

Chapter Nine

Not really the weekend from hell. It didn't rate highly on any emotional scale. Friday night, Elise made it to the hotel by eight and we had dinner with her parents, who held off mentioning grandkids for the evening—plenty of time ahead for that. Saturday, we did the usual things. Elise and her mom went shopping, while Tom and I had a couple of beers and watched the game. Correction. I watched, he listened to the roar of the crowd and my running commentary of the action. I can't even begin to imagine how frustrating it must have been for him to not be able to enjoy the simple things in life, but he didn't let it get to him. Took it on the chin, like a real man. It got me thinking about the whole gender difference aspect. I'm actually OK with shopping, if there's a reason for it, rather than the browse and buy whatever takes their fancy Elise and Darla engaged in that afternoon, just like every other trip they took. In fact, I wasn't convinced that love or hate of shopping had anything to do with being a woman or a man. Like my attitude on most things, if it served a purpose, then all well and good. If it didn't, then what was the point of wasting the time, energy and money? I think it was probably more to do with being an engineer, as George was exactly the same as the rest of us in the office, the rest of us being men.

I left Tom napping, to go and collect Elise and her mom and their dozen multi-colored bags. I even rustled up a little interest in the big reveal that followed. Elise had bought a stunning black dress—floor length and pulled in at the waist. She was quite tall and shapely, and looked mighty fine in slinky black. It was for the garden party, she said, accessorized, of course, by a pair of implausibly high-heeled black-patent sandals, and coordinating purse barely big enough to hold a lipstick.

All purchases stowed away, we settled down for a homemade meal—nothing special, just chicken and pasta. It was as we came to the end of this simple meal that Darla, in her roundabout way, raised the issue of starting a family again.

"You'll be looking to buy a house soon," she stated.

"Mom," Elise beseeched.

"Oh, Elise, sweetie, you're in your thirties now."

"And?"

"Time is *not* on your side."

Elise shook her head and started clearing the table. Darla smiled at me. She must've spotted the microscopic weak link in our defense.

"You could buy a place outright within a couple of years," she said knowledgeably. Darla had worked in real estate for a while after Elise started high school. "There are some beautiful houses in Dorchester."

I shrugged neutrally. "We like this apartment, Darla."

"But you only have the one bedroom," she said. Elise had her back turned, loading the dishwasher, making her disapproval of my engaging her mother wholly apparent. Darla reached across and squeezed my hand. I gave her a smile, but no more than that, hoping she'd let it go. She didn't, and eventually I had to agree to drive them back to their hotel before all hell broke loose. That was the problem with Darla and Elise—both refused to plainly say exactly what they meant, so arguments tended to go round the same few vague points, where getting a house in the suburbs served as a euphemism for starting a family, and feeling accomplished in getting a promotion equated to having no intention of having children, ever. I often wondered if straight talking wouldn't kill the issue once and for all.

"When are you going to have children, Elise?"

"Never, Mom."

Done.

On the matter of straight talking, once we'd safely seen Elise's parents onto their plane home, I headed for the gym—the Magda gym, that is. I'd been in there a couple of times before, and it was very well equipped, with the latest machines, two eager-beaver instructors on standby. The only staff that used the place over the weekend were security guards, maintenance crew and the sad nine-to-fivers with no life to speak of outside of work. Like me.

I snagged a free treadmill and cranked it up to a steady seven miles an hour, stuck my earphones in and switched off from the world. I ran up a good sweat, intending to get a full workout, because I really didn't want to be at home with Elise. Tom and Darla's visit had postponed the storm's arrival, but it was getting closer now. I could feel it in my bones. I slowed the treadmill, removing my earphones as I stepped off, making a beeline for the weights room. And there, pumping away on the flies, was none other than Best Western 702. I swear the gods were conspiring against me.

"I didn't know you came here," I said.

"Just joined," said 702. He heaved the arms of the machine in front of him, grunted, eased them back again, released. "The name's Rick, by the way."

"Sol," I replied. I sat on the lat pulldown, not that I used machines normally, but I wanted to get a good look at him up-close, for no other reason than curiosity, it turned out. He was still a good-looking guy, well-toned but not built, like Adam, and he was smart and funny. He finished his workout and hung around a while, telling me about the new job he was starting the following day in our accounts section, having graduated from Harvard Business School the previous year. He'd been staying in the hotel while he searched for an apartment, and hadn't realized at first I could see into his window. There was nothing bashful about his admission. He was obviously very proud of his bod, and he had every right to be, but it did nothing for me. Not anymore. We parted company outside the gym, me wishing him luck with his new job, him yet again bemused by my rejection.

Back home, Elise was reading a case brief and glanced up as I passed by on the way to the shower. I knew what was coming, and I didn't want to deal with it. My head was completely screwed as it was. I stayed in the bathroom for as long as I could without further rousing her suspicion that I was avoiding her, emerged and grabbed my iPad, quickly loading a movie. I plopped onto the sofa, aware of her eyes burning holes in my back. I listened to the tap of her pen on the table. The tapping stopped. The pen rolled.

"Are you seeing him?" she asked.

"Who?"

"The guy from the store."

I closed my eyes, forced myself to keep breathing; slow, deep, steady.

"Since last Monday you've been different," she continued.

"In what way?" I turned so I could see her. She shrugged and looked away.

"I don't know. Kind of distant, snippy."

"Snippy?" I repeated, laughing with a little too much incredulity. "Has it occurred to you that it might not be me who's acting differently?"

"Meaning?"

"Jen."

At least she had the decency to blush.

"I like Jen. We get along."

"And that's all?"

"I don't know what you're talking about."

She got up, took her case notes, and went to the bedroom, closing the door ever so gently behind her.

***

Monday.

I felt like death warmed up and was starting to think that maybe I really was coming down with something. I glanced up at the empty, dark window of Best Western 702, briefly thought about its previous occupant, conjured an image in my mind's eye of him in his smart suit, in his smart new job. He looked happy. My desk phone started ringing, ripping me from my pointless reverie. George's extension.

"Hey, George."

"Sol. We've got a problem. You need to head on over to the workshop."

Workshop. It was in actuality a massive factory, but I think Magda was trying for a more "cottage industry" image. Like Pottery Barn.

"Why? What's up?"

"The M-fifty-one dimensions don't match up to the design."

We got this from time to time with our mass-produced lines. Human error was usually the cause, and no one individual could be held accountable, considering the number of steps involved in the process between conception and production.

"OK. Send me the details in an email. I'll go now."

I hung up and grabbed my jacket.

I was halfway to the workshop before I remembered that Adam was swinging by at some point. We hadn't agreed on a time, just Monday, so as soon as I parked the car I called. Straight to voicemail. I left a message explaining I'd had to pop out and would hopefully be back for lunch, and went inside to find out what was going on.

As I'd suspected, it was nothing more than a mistyped number, but finding it took the rest of the morning. Whenever the opportunity arose, I checked my phone for missed calls—there was next to no signal in the factory, on account of all the equipment. As soon as I stepped outside the call came.

"Talk about star-crossed lovers," Adam said.

I registered "lovers" first, the rest of it taking a little longer to filter through. I waited for him to continue.

"I've got to see the police this afternoon. Make a statement about the student who died."

"Oh. Not fun." My stomach knotted tight. I felt bad for him. "Are you free this evening?"

"No can do. I'm flying to Montreal for a conference."

He paused. I could think of nothing to say.

"I'll be back on Thursday. You want to catch a movie, or something?"

Elise's damned garden party.

"I can't," I said, the words accompanied by a sigh.

"OK. What about Friday? You free then?"

I was, but you know that feeling, when fate's waving a red flag in your face? That's what I was getting. Mother Nature thought this was a bad idea, and who am I to argue with a force that can take out entire continents with one puff of her mighty lungs?

"Yeah, I'm free Friday. I can be free all day."

Valiant engineer, poking the face of fear in the eye. That's me.

"Cool," Adam said. I could hear in his voice that he was smiling. "I'll call you, OK?"

"OK."

I hung up and drove back to Magda, feeling a whole lot better than I had first thing that morning.

***

And call me he did. Every day, at least three times.

"Hey, handsome."

Huh. Too familiar. Too…permanent.

"Hey," I replied stoically.

"What's up?"

How did he know? I laughed, disconcerted. "Nothing. I'm fine."

"Busy?"

"A little."

"In that case I'll let you go."

"No." Too needy? Well, he did call me handsome.

"OK," he said. We both laughed. "I miss you."

"No you don't."

"Yeah, I do."

"How? We've had dinner and half-sex."

"It was great half-sex though. I can't wait for the second course."

I moved my phone away from my ear and stared at it, mostly to check the call was for real. I put it back to my ear. "We need to talk."

"Yeah."

We did need to talk. My life was hanging in the balance.

In between phone calls, he sent me sext messages—not the photographic type, just words.

> *Made my very own loofah in the shower thinking of you. x*

Oh really? I typed back. *Did you know loofahs can grow up to two feet long? x*

Uh huh? was what I got back, with a winking smiley face.

Ha, yeah. Nearly thirty-one and texting like a teenager in love. Go figure.

What I didn't factor into all of the fun and games was that it constituted documentary evidence for my newly paranoid wife. She'd never snooped on me before, so I had no reason to think she would then, or else I'd have made sure not to let my phone out of my sight.

Thursday morning, as she left for work, she turned back at the door, a warning glint in her eye.

"If you fuck this up for me tonight, Sol, so help me…"

I snapped. I'd had enough.

"What do you think I'm gonna do, Elise? Tell Rory you're screwing one of his paralegals? His *female* paralegals?"

"Don't you dare make this about me," she yelled. She was angry, verging on hysterical. "I've seen the messages from *him*."

I nodded slowly. I wasn't going to deny it, though her reaction indicated she expected me to.

"Why don't you close the door?" I suggested. "Clear the air before we go to work?"

"I'm late." She left, a sob lingering in the echo of the slam of the door.

We did the garden party. It was…pleasant. Jen was there, with her sister playing the part of chaperone. Elise consorted with the other partners, laughing politely, complimenting them and/or their wives on outfits and hairdos. I followed in her wake, endeavoring to be masculine, handsome, hetero.

We did the garden party. And then we went home and argued goodbye.

Chapter Ten

We'd arranged to meet at the entrance to Boston Common on the corner of Charles and Boylston, in running gear, and I hadn't really thought it through. I didn't have a change of clothes with me, and had no plans to return home before Sunday. That was, however, not the foremost thing on my mind as I leaned against the railing, watching Adam all the way across the street. He was wearing a light gray tee, shorts of a slightly darker gray, his olive skin glowing in the early morning sun, his lip and chin sporting a day or two's stubble. Hard to believe, but his hair had grown enough in a week to be tousled, a stray lock punctuating the smooth slope of his forehead. He looked so damned hot, and not because he'd jogged all the way from his apartment, as evidenced by him being slightly out of breath. I half-considered telling him to forget about the run. There were far better things to expend our energy on. He came right up to me and kissed me tenderly. People passed by. My world spun wildly out of control. I kept hold of the railing a little longer, just breathing in his scent.

"Hey," he said. "How's things?"

"Can I answer that later?"

He examined my rueful smile through thoughtful eyes. "Is it bad?"

"Depends how you define bad." I stepped off. He kept apace, and as we entered the common, we increased our speed to a gentle jog. "How was the conference?" I asked.

"Really good. It was mostly workshops—scriptwriters, directors, producers—and research panels. I learned a lot."

"Such as?"

"How much I miss you already."

I chanced a glance his way. He met my gaze and gave me a big, genuine smile. I lost my rhythm and stumbled. He put out an arm to steady me. I found myself smiling back. Crazy little thing.

"Did it go OK with the cops?"

"Yeah." He turned to face front, staring into the distance. I'd hit a still-raw nerve. "The pathologist says she's confident it was suicide."

I'd read the reports in the local press, and it was tragic. The victim, if that was the right term for it, was a nineteen-year-old from Washington DC, known to have been suffering from depression. According to the papers, he'd hanged himself from the light fixture in the two-bed dorm, having previously taken a massive overdose of sleeping pills, along with a significant quantity of alcohol. His roommate found him, ran out of the dorm shouting for help, and was heard by "a member of faculty," who called 911, that member of faculty being Adam. I could see it had hit him hard, but he was still coping a hell of a lot better than I would have done.

We jogged around the perimeter of the common, a distance of around a mile, and slowed to a walk.

"What happened?" he asked.

"With Elise?"

He nodded.

"She saw the texts on my phone."

"Ah, shit."

"Yeah. There was a garden party at the law firm last night. She told me not to fuck it up for her, but I can't do it anymore."

I'd said it with conviction, like I knew I was doing the right thing, but my mind was wracked with doubt. Adam and I barely knew each other, and the stakes were high. There was still the possibility to carry on as before, go back home on Sunday and continue with my sham marriage, the masquerade that was my life, but did I want that? Risk losing everything, or give up the one and only thing that felt real to me.

"I have a proposal for you," Adam said. We shifted up a gear, setting off on a second circuit. "You want to hear it now, or wait?"

"No. Let's hear it."

"Move in with me."

Wow. That was unexpected, not that I'd had time to speculate on what I was expecting.

"Are you serious?"

"Very."

I started working through the excuses in my head. It was less than two weeks since we'd met. We'd only had one date. I was married. Then there was the apartment, Elise, my career…

"If you're worried about the financial side of it, don't be. The apartment comes with the job, and I already checked on the rules about cohabiting.

"You did?"

Of course he did.

"And you don't need to decide right away."

Fit as I was, I didn't have enough breath for a discussion like that while running, and in any case we'd found our groove, so we continued in silence. It was a great feeling, running together. Once again I was struck by how comfortable it was, familiar. Normally I'd run alone, and I can't say I'd ever craved a running buddy. I can't say I'd ever craved anyone the way I did Adam. He stopped to deal with a cramp, bending over and rubbing his calf. A couple of younger women walked by and glanced our way.

"Nice ass," one of them called.

Adam laughed graciously. "Thanks."

I figured I might as well take a look too. He peered up at me, still smiling.

"Yeah," I said, in agreement. He had a really nice ass. I couldn't wait to get my hands on it.

We were at the junction of the path that cut through the middle of the common, back toward the street.

"You want to carry on?" he asked. I shook my head. We veered off, taking the shortcut, stopping at a convenience store to buy a bottle of water on the way back to Adam's place. It was a one-and-half-liter bottle, and we shared both it and a discussion of the different weights and measures in the US, compared to back home in the UK, our geeky conversation granting me an opening to ask Adam about his accent.

"My parents are Kiwis, but I was born and bred in London."

"That's crazy." I'd have laid money on him being a native New Zealander. Well, Australian at any rate. Close enough.

"They've got pretty strong accents. I guess they must've rubbed off on me."

That's what I hoped I'd be doing soon. He handed me the water.

"What about you?" he asked. "Where are you from? Up north somewhere?"

"Semi-rural Yorkshire." It was as concise a location as his "born and bred in London." South Yorkshire might not have been big by US standards, but it was the largest county in England. He seemed satisfied with my response for now, more interested in watching me accidentally tip half a pint of ice-cold water down my front. I gasped. He gave me that lopsided grin.

"That was sexy," he said.

"It was bloody cold!"

He laughed and put a hot arm around me. I screwed the lid back on the bottle, put my arm around him too, and that's how we stayed for the entire walk back.

We didn't fight about who got the shower first. We stripped off and stepped under the powerful jets together. He pulled me close, and we kissed hungrily, open-mouthed, biting, sucking, exploring, tongues reveling in the lubricating effect of the steamy hot water. The soft rasping of his stubble made me tingle all over. I was completely overwhelmed by his scent, the heat of his skin, the power of his body against mine. We were both so hard that we grabbed each other's cocks and jerked off, our fists banging together in desperation for release. His grip was like iron, and he worked me hard and fast—just what I needed—so much better than going it alone. I tried to focus on keeping the same rhythm. His dick was slightly bigger than mine and felt familiar and different at the same time. I liked that. It reminded me that I was with someone else. I was with him. Adam. *My* Captain Impatient.

I withdrew from the kissing to look at what I was doing to him, what he was doing to me. He was watching too and that was such a turn-on. His eyelids fluttered, the goofy expression giving away how close he was, how much he was enjoying it. I returned my gaze to our cocks, fascinated by how they every so often touched tips, flesh warriors bowing in preparation of a fight to the death. The blood was pulsing hard through him, and I increased my grip against the tension of his orgasm shooting up, the white pearly strings rising in arcs, falling and nestling into my pubic hair, before being washed away. I experienced a brief panic that he was now left to finish me off when he was done, but he was still thrusting into my hand and had returned to kissing me, his tongue ramming deep into my mouth as his hand tightened around me, squeezing the panic out of me, tipping me over the edge. I shot a great stream onto his belly, followed by another, and another.

I caught my breath within his kisses. It was without a doubt the most intense climax I'd had in a long time, and I was still riding the wave, only partly aware of his other hand on my back, keeping me from buckling at the knees.

We didn't release each other right away, because it still felt good. We were both sporting porn-star semis, and everything had slowed down, our kissing now less hungry, yet just as deep as before.

"I'm going to make us brunch in a while," he said. "How does that sound?"

It sounded great. I was starving, but I didn't want him to let go of me. He cautiously moved his hand from my back, searching out the bottle of shower gel from the shelf behind me, flipped it open one-handed and squeezed a dollop of the purple gloop onto my chest. I held out my hand, and he deposited some more on my palm. We massaged and washed each other at the same time, and could have started up the whole process again, both of us rising to the occasion, but we didn't. We had three full days of being together ahead of us, time to get to know each other properly, take it nice and slow, exercise some patience! So we just washed each other, making sure we were thoroughly clean, everywhere. Adam washed my hair. I washed his, and we laughed at our dicks doing that mating dance of theirs.

We stayed in the shower until our fingers wrinkled, didn't bother drying off, just wrapped towels around our waists that soon worked themselves free. Adam made coffee and French toast, and we ate naked, feeding and teasing each other by offering a bite then snatching it away. I took a mouthful of coffee, didn't swallow, put my mouth around his dick, letting the warmth of the liquid bring him back to life. What a thing this was, in his kitchen, sharing brunch and sucking him off. He tasted so good, and I figured I owed him from the week before. I took some more coffee, lowered my mouth right down till my lips touched the surrounding flesh, slowly easing back up. I swallowed, descended, scraping my teeth over the silky-smooth skin. I could tell he was watching me again, and I changed position to give him a better view, reaching for my own dick, hanging heavy with need. I wanted to be inside him—I wasn't sure how he'd feel about that. I ran my fingers along his crack to see how he responded.

"You want to fuck me?" he asked. I nodded. "Here?"

In the kitchen. It was going to be the shortest fuck ever if we did it there, and the condoms were in the bedroom. We adjourned. I must admit I was a little nervous, and also aware that it was being in his bedroom that triggered it. Now I had a handle on that part, I could maybe start to understand why, though not right at that moment.

I hate to admit it, but stress put a real downer on the proceedings, and I'd well and truly gone off the boil. Adam noticed my change of mood right away.

"What's up?" he asked. I glanced down, felt my face heat up.

"Nothing," I said, trying to cover my embarrassment with an over-exaggerated sigh. "I'm sorry, but can we have a time out?"

He didn't question it, just opened a drawer and passed me a pair of shorts and a T-shirt.

I sat on the edge of the bed to put the shorts on. "Sorry," I said again.

"Chill."

I was trying to. No way was I going to let these panic attacks, or whatever they were, ruin our weekend. Maybe if we just stayed out of the bedroom? Didn't really make for much in the way of debauchery. Or sleep.

It turned out that's how we played it—plenty of debauchery, everywhere but the bedroom, which we entered only to sleep, so not very much over the course of those three days. A favorite was sucking each other off in the shower. Adam looked unbelievably sexy with water cascading over him, the droplets glistening silver pearls against his dark complexion. I think I spent more time in a vacant daze, watching him get wet, than I did touching him. A close second was lying together on the sofa and kissing, with or without clothes. I even enjoyed lying in the bed with him for a short while on Saturday morning, until the jitters set in again.

The intimacy was incredible, but we also spent a lot of time just talking about anything and everything. No agenda—

whatever came to mind. We laughed a lot too. For me that was what set apart this thing we had from every other relationship I'd experienced. Elise and I had sex for release, we talked about work, we went shopping for groceries. I don't recall the last time we laughed. Very telling.

Adam and I had fun together. We got the giggles, we laughed till we cried. Sometimes we'd be caught up in a deep, serious kiss and we'd start fooling around, in a non-sexual sense. At one point we were in the kitchen. I was making us something to eat, while Adam opened a couple of beers, the arm with the tattoo closest to me.

"What is it?" I asked.

"A QR code."

"OK." Seemed a strange thing to have tattooed on your arm. "Why?"

"I'm not supposed to tell anyone," he said very seriously, "but I think I can trust you to keep this to yourself."

"Uh huh?" I knew he was winding me up, but I went along with it.

"Yeah. I used to work for this secret government agency, as a spy."

"Is that so?"

"A tough job, but someone's got to do it." He tapped the tattoo with his index finger. "These babies were in case any of us got captured. If they're scanned they trigger a security alert and send a GPS signal to pinpoint our location."

I shook my head, faking dismay. He grinned at me.

"It was a silly drunken idea a few of us had one night—tattoo a barcode linking to your Grindr profile. A hot guy comes your way, scans your arm, saves your details on his phone."

"Did it work?"

"It used to, but I'm not on Grindr anymore."

"Shame," I said, retrieving my phone from the side and holding it up, pretending I was about to scan the tattoo. I didn't even have an app for that. Adam snatched the phone and grabbed me around the waist in an attempt to fell me. I escaped his evil clutches, ran straight across the hall, leapt the sofa, and we spent a crazy couple of minutes edging one way and then the other, just like kids playing chase. Surprise, surprise, he got impatient and vaulted the couch too, getting me around the knees and wrestling me to the floor. I had the giggles again, our antics having put me in mind of the Freddie Mercury video for "I Was Born To Love You," whereby he chases a woman through the rooms of a house, or a set that looks like a house, at least. Quite what he was intending to do with her once he caught her I really don't know, but that was another moment of passion potential suspended as I recounted my mother's response to me telling her—how being "gay like Freddie Mercury" was a one way ticket to dying from *The* AIDS.

"She does know you have to fuck someone with HIV to catch it, doesn't she?" Adam asked.

I raised an eyebrow, choosing not to comment. I don't suppose he meant it the way I heard it, but he was right. Three days together and we'd done everything but fuck.

Chapter Eleven

The apartment was in darkness when I arrived back late Sunday night. I assumed by the flickering of the TV screen on the bedroom wall that Elise was asleep. I preferred not to watch TV in bed—something else I'd discovered Adam and I had in common—but Elise said she liked the noise, especially when sleeping alone. At least I knew where I stood.

I lingered in the hallway, casting my eye over the dark silhouettes and shadows of our apartment—my home of the past eight years—for the first time acknowledging how little of me resided there. I'd never been the type to collect things simply for their sentimental value. I didn't get attached to books, or CDs. My memory was all the record I needed of those important moments in my life, and to be honest there wasn't that much to catalog—my graduation, our wedding…

There was something on the breakfast bar…Well what do you know? Three days and I was right back in the habit of thinking in my native tongue. I wandered over, flicked on the lamp, saw what it was. A birthday present, from Elise. I'd forgotten the next day was my birthday. Amazing. I'd spent much of the last year worrying about the significance of turning thirty-one, because a thirty-year-old screwing a guy in his twenties seemed far less perverted than a guy in his thirties going after a twenty-two-year-old. That's how it sounded in my head, where it had become such a big deal that I couldn't believe it had slipped my mind so completely.

On top of the small, gift-wrapped box was a white envelope, which I assumed at first to be a card. I picked it up and turned it over, wondering all the while why Elise had left it for me before the actual day. Maybe she was going away on business.

Or maybe not.

The envelope was too flimsy to contain a card. I lifted the unstuck flap and pulled out the sheet of paper within. A "Dear John" letter—kind of, as in the words made it clear this was the end. It was my eviction notice.

I don't know how long I remained there, reading over that letter, again, and again, waiting, anticipating something. I felt nothing. No remorse, no regret, no sadness. She wanted me to go right away, expected to wake up to an empty apartment in the morning, but after three days of physical exertion and very little sleep, I was incapable of going anywhere. I grabbed some blankets and collapsed on the sofa.

The next thing I was aware of was Elise banging stuff down in the kitchen. I kept my eyes closed and listened to the intermittent sniffs and mucus coughs of someone trying to stifle their tears. It wasn't that I didn't care, but her sorrow was misplaced. Eight years together, an apartment that had held its value, successful careers—we'd done well to keep it up for so long. I pulled the blankets around me and got up, slowly turning to watch her going about her morning ritual, refusing to look my way.

"Elise, I—"

She cut me off. "I don't want to hear it."

"You don't know what I was going to say."

"I'm not interested."

"You mean you can't face the truth."

She put her hand to her face and made a dash for the bathroom. I followed in my bulky blanket toga, watching her from the doorway, as she mopped at her eyes, trying to save her mascara. I addressed her reflection.

"I'm truly sorry. I didn't plan for this to happen, I swear, but now it has there's no going back. We knew it would come to this. We both knew."

"I didn't," she objected.

I stayed silent. I wasn't going to argue with denial.

"Do you love him?"

"I've only known him for two weeks. Not even that, really."

"That doesn't answer my question."

I didn't have an answer to give. Did I love him? If I judged it on the basis of a decade spent playing the field versus two weeks of desiring no one but him, then yes, perhaps I did. But that was by the by. Whether Adam and I had a future or not, the marriage was over. Any guilt I felt for my part was being overridden by the fact that Elise was more upset about what it meant for her career and her relationship with her mother than the demise of "us." She turned to face me, her eyes bloodshot, still more tears trickling from the corners. She flicked one away. As it fell, it sparkled in the wispy sunlight weaving its way through the slats of the window blind.

"Yeah," I said. "I think I do."

The admission was nothing to do with my sudden fidelity. Watching Elise, trying to pull herself together so she could make it to the office, carry on pretending everything was OK, being something she wasn't? That's what made me accept the truth. I could almost hear myself making that speech to the board.

I'm gay. My marriage is over. I've met someone new and I think I might love him. You can tell our investors to go to hell, or fire me. Whatever.

Elise made to pass me in the doorway. I put my hand on her arm.

"I'll go today," I said.

"You don't need to."

I wasn't sure where yet, but I was going. Elise gave me a sad smile and kissed me lightly.

"Happy birthday," she whispered. I watched her gather herself together and leave for work.

I hadn't even got as far as sagging in relief when the phone started ringing, and I knew who it would be. I shuffled, Geisha style, across the apartment.

"Hello, Mum," I answered the phone, trying to sound bright and cheery.

"Good morning, Solomon. It is morning, isn't it?"

"Yep. It's just gone seven thirty." I needed to get my ass in gear.

"I won't keep you, darling. I just wanted to wish you a happy birthday. Do you have anything nice planned for the day?"

Leaving my wife, booking into the YMCA…

"I'm thirty-one, Mother. It's not exactly worth celebrating. And I'm at work."

"Not *all* day, surely?"

"Well, no, obviously."

"You should get that well-paid wife of yours to take you out to dinner."

Another of the grandparent-wannabe snipes.

"Yeah, there's an idea," I said through gritted teeth. "I'm gonna have to go, Mum."

"All right. Have a lovely day. Love to Elise."

"Same to you and Dad. Bye."

***

Flowers. In my office. Lots, and lots of flowers. And not just any old flowers. Yellow daffodils, nodding a courteous greeting as I passed to get to my desk, and back again to fill the coffee machine.

Tap-tap-tap-tap.

"Come," I called, heading for the door to rescue George from her imminent collision with my myriad new friends.

"Oh!" she said.

Oh, indeed.

"Where in the heck did all these come from?"

I took a breath, opened my mouth, closed it again, let go of the breath, frowned, and said, "Have a seat, George. I need to tell you something."

She sat. I made the coffee and joined her. She studied me, patiently waiting to hear what I had to say.

"OK," I said, aware of the slight tremor in my voice. My palms were sweaty. "You know I'm gay, right?"

Those little beady eyes narrowed, staring straight into mine, her mouth drawn tight. She took some coffee. "Right," she said.

I nodded, pleased she hadn't argued the point. "I'm going to tell the board."

Her tongue rolled thoughtfully across her lips, and she chewed as if a matchstick were perched in the corner of her mouth.

"Sol." She let a loud sigh go. "Oh, Sol." She shook her head. "I've known you a long time, and you're a very talented engineer. Magda—"

"Yeah, I know, George. But I'd rather quit than carry on pretending to be something I'm not. The thing is—" How to say it?

"You and Elise?" she prompted.

"We're over."

"I'm sorry."

I shrugged. "I'm not. See, I met this guy…" I smiled at the thought, deciding it wouldn't help any to tell her I'd only met him a fortnight ago. "In the store, and we just kind of hit it off." I indicated the profusion of yellow filling the room. "He did this."

"What a sap!" George was all southern sensibility, not a trace of romance in her, though I was inclined to agree. Filling someone's office with flowers was…*sappy*! And not what I'd have expected from Adam at all. We were a lot alike—tough, masculine, testosterone and manly pursuits. I was definitely not a hearts-and-flowers guy, and I could see George still struggling to reconcile.

"He asked me what I missed about home—he's English too. I said I missed seeing daffodils on my birthday."

"It's your birthday?"

Darn it.

"I've been trying to weasel that out of HR since you started here."

"You know me, George. I don't like a fuss."

Past tense would have been more accurate, as I was flattered by the flowers, I must admit. However, the prospect of enduring the usual round of birthday pleasantries and gooey cake wasn't one I relished.

George picked up one of the bunches, sniffed the bell of a daffodil and grimaced. I held in my laughter.

"They don't smell of anything," she said.

It was a curious observation. I could understand why she'd made it, though. I'd put her in a very difficult position. She'd been my champion at Magda, pushing me forward so I could make my mark. She believed in me, or who she thought was me. I'd let her down, not by being what I was, but because I'd made a liar of her. The tension between us was new, and tangible. Another knock came at the door.

"Come," I called.

I watched as the door opened very slowly, no clue as to who was on the other side yet. I frowned in puzzlement. George was watching too, as a bottle of Champagne came into view. I recognized those fingers, *his* fingers, wrapped around the neck of the bottle like they'd been wrapped around me for much of the past three days. My heart went into a canter. Adam stepped inside.

"Hey, oh!" He smiled at George. "Sorry," he said. "I'll just…" He took a step away.

George looked him over, turned back to me.

"This him?"

"Uh huh."

She nodded.

"Think I'll leave y'all to it," she said. She got up. I followed her to the door. She paused to examine us, standing side by side.

"Give me a call when you go upstairs. I'll come with you."

I smiled in gratitude, but this was my problem, not hers. "Thanks," I said. "I'm sure I'll be OK."

She squeezed my arm affectionately. "Give me a call," she repeated. She glanced up at Adam, gave him a nod that looked a lot like approval, and left, closing the door behind her.

"They arrived then?" he said, looking around my office.

"Yeah, they arrived. You! Are insane!"

He grinned and put his arms around me, hauling me in. I let him kiss me, but I wasn't happy about it, not in my office. I liked my job. I'd prefer not to lose it, if possible. I freed myself from his embrace, returned to my desk and picked up the coffee cups. It was something to do.

"So Elise threw me out," I said casually, as if I were delivering a bland weather related statement. *Turned out nice again.*

"She did, huh?"

"Yeah. I'm going to go book into the Best Western later."

"Why?"

I turned and looked at him. "Because I have nowhere to live?"

He raked his fingers through his hair. He'd raised his guard.

"Can you help me out a little here?" he asked.

"Sure. What's the problem?"

"You're going to book into a hotel."

"Yeah. It's just across the street." I pointed out the window.

"It's only a train ride from Emerson."

"And?"

"I already made the offer."

"That's not the same. I just need..." I shrugged. "Time. I need time."

"Then what the hell was the weekend all about?"

"Adam, I…" There it was: a flash of anger. Impatience. And more than that, pain. "Look, we've known each other two weeks. My marriage has just ended. It's too soon for me to—"

"OK. I get it."

The door slammed behind him, the gust setting off the daffodils in a Mexican wave right around the room.

***

I did as I'd said I would. I booked into the Best Western, and as they handed me the key my heart sank. Room…

…701. At least it wasn't 702, though I could still have zipwired from my bed to my desk. Awesome.

That was as good as my evening got, sitting on an unforgiving hotel bed, creating mental drafts for an inter-building hydraulic cable system. By nine thirty, I'd given up on Adam calling. I went for a shower, crawled under the scratchy covers and turned out the light. Happy fucking birthday to me.

Chapter Twelve

I spoke to the board, in George's presence, on Tuesday. They were very supportive, which surprised us both, but then the issue had never been with Magda's directors. Rather, it was their investors, or one in particular, and I could fully appreciate the board's dilemma, duty-bound to uphold anti-discrimination law when it could put the firm in financial jeopardy. So many of our competitors had gone out of business already, and I felt dreadfully responsible for putting them in this situation. Magda was one of those companies with a "traditional family values" byline, which I'd known when I applied for the job, not that I'd ever figured out how traditional family values had anything to do with the design of innovative office furniture. But anyway, I didn't ask how they intended to take things forward. Indeed, I was avoiding thinking about the future at all—getting through the present was challenge enough. Too many unknowns. How long was I going to stay in a hotel? How long before Elise chucked my stuff in the trash? Did I still have my promotion? Was Adam ever going to call?

After work, I went down to use the gym, where Rick was on the chest fly again—funny to think he'd almost been my next-door neighbor. We worked out together, chatting about his first week at Magda. He was part of the team responsible for analyzing the company's assets and setting investment priorities. I suppose it was a natural progression of the conversation that I ended up telling him about my "coming out" ordeal and the troublesome investor. He listened without comment, or, should I say, without vocalizing his disapproval, but it was obvious from his face what he thought. On some things, those ten years between us really did matter. I doubted he'd ever see the inside of a closet—probably didn't even use one for his clothes. It was easy to forget what those who had gone before had done for us. I thought back to Calvin's political rants about Stonewall and the importance of Pride marches, Matthew Shepard's legacy—it was all so detached and alien to me back then. And for all that Cal was aggressive, unfaithful and shallow, I couldn't fault his activism and passion. It was a life lesson Rick could benefit from—knock that sneering, "I'm gay, so what?" expression right off his face. I didn't say any of this aloud, of course. These were bitter, regretful thoughts, misdirected at Rick in an attempt to push away a much darker realization. *James died for guys like you. Like me.*

As Rick was leaving, he let slip that the CEO had already given the order to put out feelers for alternative backing, and I was moderately relieved to hear that, but in truth I didn't care much. My daffodils were starting to wilt, as was my determination.

Wednesday was more of the same. I was close enough to work that I could've got up at eight and still arrived early, yet there I was, six fifteen, staring sleeplessly at the ceiling, trying to ignore the backache and misery. It was so damned frustrating. I gave up, had a shower and went to the office.

At nine o'clock, I had my first official meeting with "my" team—George and I had agreed to split the old team in half and take two new guys each, except one of my new guys was a gal. She reminded me of Elise. I tried not to hold it against her, not that I had much opportunity to dwell on it, as it turned out to be a busy day, filled with reorganizing the design office to accommodate the extra drawing boards and Apple Macs.

The physical activity must have done something for me, as I slept right through to my Thursday morning alarm. A glimmer of hope on the horizon, I showered, had breakfast in the hotel, and strolled over to the Magda building, where my team sparkled with enthusiasm, all go-getter attitude and eagerness to please. The novelty soon wore off for me, though they were still buzzing at quitting time—I swear I'd never consumed so many lattes in one work day. Needing to burn off those calories, I followed it up with a full cardio workout in the basement gym. Rick wasn't around, which was disappointing, not that I was healing any, but I enjoyed his company; he was easygoing and interesting. And he was a distraction.

Friday, after another sleepless night and clearing my office of most of the daffodils, cracks started to appear in the concrete of my resolve, pieces breaking off under the pressure of the corrosion within. Five days. That's how long I'd been single, but it was more than enough for me. I considered calling Elise, not to seek reconciliation, nor even to ask if I could sleep on the sofa. I'd put off calling her all week, hoping to have a definitive timescale for when I'd be coming for the rest of my things, though I knew if I called I'd be spending Friday evening carting my junk from the car to my hotel room, only to have to do it all over again when I found somewhere more permanent. No, I knew how I wanted to spend my Friday night, and it didn't involve being bitched at or ignored by my soon-to-be ex-wife.

Straight after work I took the Red Line up to Park Street, only calling him when I was outside the station—stupid, I know. Voicemail. I called again. Still voicemail. I was there already, so I figured I had nothing to lose. I mean, what was the worst that could happen? He'd be out of town again, or teaching, maybe, or out with friends, in which case I could just get right back on the train and return to staring at a Best Western ceiling.

Or he could be with another guy.

The realization hit me as I climbed the steps to his apartment. I could hear music from inside, so I knew he was home. I raised my hand to knock, hesitated. I couldn't deal with even the thought of him being with someone else, but for as long as I didn't knock, that was all it would be; a thought, a suspicion. Why in hell's name was I here? Definitely some form of self-torture. Oh well, nothing ventured…

I knocked. Loudly, to make sure I could be heard over the music. It stopped.

"It's open." His voice sounded muffled, and I got the feeling he'd been expecting someone else. I decided to stay where I was.

"It's me," I said, then added, "Sol." Just in case.

The door opened. A waft of cologne came my way. He was clean-shaven and dressed smartly, for him—an open-necked shirt, blazer and slacks. Shoes, not boots.

"Hey," I said, disarmed by his silence. "I owe you an apology. Again."

He checked his phone screen. "For?" he asked carelessly. It was faked, I hoped.

"For…"

Actually, why was I apologizing? All I'd done was book into a hotel. Call me old-fashioned, but two weeks is a little hasty for moving in with the self-proclaimed "love of your life."

I said, "If you'd given me a chance to explain—"

"You assumed I was asking you to move in as my lover."

"Weren't you?"

"You needed somewhere to stay."

"You honestly thought we could be roommates and nothing else?"

"I was under the impression we were already more than that."

"Which is exactly my point. I can't just step out of eight years of marriage and into a relationship with you."

"With me specifically?"

"With anyone! But now you come to mention it. It's too fast. I mean, what's the big rush? We hardly know each other."

He checked his phone again and breathed out heavily. Impatiently. I was stopping him from leaving. I could see that. I turned to walk away, all set to offer a vague "I'll be in touch" dismissal over my shoulder, and was stopped short by the sight of someone coming up the steps—a slim, auburn-haired, good-looking guy. He gave me a curious smile. I nodded in acknowledgement and left without looking back. If everything I'd said were true, then why did it hurt so much?

I was halfway to the station when I heard the sound of someone running up the street, feet pounding, getting closer and closer. Wishful thinking, right? It wasn't going to be him. Why would it be him? He was going out for the evening, with his hot date, and I…was going back to my lousy hotel room to spend the night alone. I had only myself to blame. The runner stepped off the curb to go wide and back up again a few yards in front of me. No. Not him. Ah, crap.

Worse still, a train was leaving as I arrived at the station. God only knew how long I'd be hanging around before the next one. I flopped miserably onto a bench and did a quick recap of the past two weeks and five days: accosted in the store by gorgeous guy, dinner date with the same, followed by inexplicable panic attack, job promotion, awesome weekend of sex and laughter, kicked out by wife, dumped, homeless, sitting in a subway on a Friday night. Was it any wonder I was so damn tired? I let my eyes close and listened to the conversation happening on the next seat along. Two women, discussing where they were headed for their evening of fun and frivolity, the words fading in and out, someone sitting down next to me. I opened my eyes again to find Adam at my side.

"Didn't you hear me?" he asked.

I stared at him dumbly.

"I was shouting to you all down the street. I thought I'd missed you."

"Apparently not." I was thinking of the guy outside his apartment. "Did you ditch your date?"

"My date?"

"The redhead?"

"Oh!" He laughed nervously. "Marcus? He wasn't my date."

"No?"

"No. He's a colleague. He stopped by to pick up some papers."

"And the fancy get-up?"

He looked sheepish. "I was on my way across town to see someone."

The train was pulling into the station. I got up.

"You getting this?" I asked.

"That depends if you are."

"I was planning to."

"Then I guess I am too."

I moved toward the now stationary train.

"Or we could go back to mine?" Adam suggested.

"I thought you said—ah!" Now I got it. I sighed in exasperation. "Why couldn't you just say that?"

Adam smiled and rolled his eyes. "Because you didn't give me a chance, as usual."

I took a breath, ready to protest. Who was it who stormed out of my office? Not me, no siree! Though I had to admit in principle he was correct.

"So, what do you think?" he prompted.

"About?"

"Coming home with me."

What did I think? I had no idea.

"Why didn't you call?" I asked. Because that was obviously the most important question of the moment.

"Why didn't *you* call?"

An equally good question. The train was about to depart. I made a dash for the doors, grabbing Adam by the hand and pulling him on with me. He just made it through the gap. The doors hissed shut.

"Yeah," I said. "I'll come home with you."

He frowned. "So where are we going?"

"To get my things and check out."

***

I'd already paid for the room for the night, so there was no need to rush. We packed my belongings into the one suitcase I'd brought with me—a crinkled heap of shirts and ties and a couple of pairs of pants—and put it by the door ready to take out to my car.

I don't quite know what happened next, but I was suddenly lying flat on my back on the bed, Adam on top of me, attempting to pin down my arms. I instinctively fought back.

"Just relax," he said, quietly but firmly. He stooped to kiss me, the gentlest pressure of his soft, warm lips on mine. I was breathing too fast. It wasn't that I didn't want to. I was actually thinking it was a good idea—less complicated, easier to deal with, especially as my previous visits to his bedroom had been nothing short of disastrous. So why was I still fighting it?

"I need to shower," I said, struggling against him. He released me.

"Are you worried about losing control?" he asked.

I didn't reply, feeling painfully self-conscious with his intense gaze following me across the room to the en suite. I set the shower running and undressed, watching my reflection mist over in the mirror above the wash basin. I'd fared poorly in my short life as a singleton, and I looked a sorry sight, with dark rings under my eyes, my hair falling over my face, my skin even paler than usual. Sad to say, with the guy of my dreams waiting just the other side of the wall, but my self-esteem was at an all-time low. I didn't know if I was ready. If I'd ever be ready.

"Want a hand in there?"

I closed my eyes, laughing in spite of myself. I felt his arms slide around me, his lips nuzzle in between my cheek and shoulder.

"You're still dressed," I said. Not much of a protest, and not very convincing with the evidence rising before me. He released me and took off his clothes.

"Better?"

I nodded and we squeezed into the shower stall together. Once there, he washed me, smoothing the soapy cloth over my body as if I were a delicate babe, his eyes remaining locked with mine, though we were both fully aroused and raring to go. I appreciated what he was doing, showing me he could slow it down if that's what I needed, and I did need that—in every other part of our rapidly blossoming relationship. As for the sex? If I had time to think, I'd screw up, lose the moment. I reached down to fondle his dick and balls to indicate I was ready, whether it were true or not. We finished showering and wrapped ourselves in towels, returning to the bed, where he waited for me to take the lead. Yet again I floundered. What was this thing with him and me and beds?

"You OK?" he asked. I attempted a smile. He sat on the edge of the mattress and beckoned me closer. I complied. I felt my towel fall away and tried to focus on the sensation of his hands and lips roaming over my body.

That was my other worry, of course. How two typical alpha males—tops, if you like—did this. I guessed we could take turns in the longer term. In the shorter, Adam had the condom out of the packet and was already rolling it onto my throbbing hard-on. That was his doing, for while my mind had been taunting me with doubts, he'd been caressing my ass and sucking me. He climbed onto his knees, pausing to give me a deep, lingering kiss, his hand still stroking my dick, his own jutting into my hip. He released me.

"Ready, handsome?"

I watched him turn his back and rest his hands on the wall at the top of the bed, his balls hanging like a ripe pear ready for picking, his firm buttocks covered in soft dark hair, his hole puckered, waiting. He wiggled his ass. It made me laugh and broke the tension between us.

"Aw, come on, Sol. I'm horny as hell here."

Now I was ready. I spotted the lube he'd left on the bed, squeezed some onto my fingers and for the fun of it into the top of his crack, giggling as he jumped at the coldness.

"So cruel," he said, his voice deep and husky with desire.

"I know. I couldn't resist."

I knelt behind him and smeared the lube down, skimming over his hole, watching him drop one hand to work his dick.

"I'll take care of that," I said, pushing the hand away and replacing it with my own. I'm not that skilled with both hands when it comes to most things, but I was pretty adept when it came to foreplay, the fingers of my right hand brushing against his already opening hole, my left pumping him. I pushed a finger inside; he resisted for a second, and relaxed. I moved in and out, watching his shoulders tense and drop, waiting until I thought he was ready for more. He started to push back onto my hand, repositioning himself. There were some seriously animal-like sounds coming from him, guttural utterances of pleasure, goading me on. I went for a second finger, then a third. He was wide open, as happy receiving as he was giving.

I shuffled closer, positioned the head of my achingly hard dick and pushed, knowing he would close around me. That was the toughest part, when all I wanted to do was ram hard into his ass, but I'd learned for myself just how unpleasant it was to be on the receiving end—unless the guy was into S and M, and I hadn't noticed any handcuffs lying around Adam's place. He relaxed again, and I pushed deeper, giving him a moment to ease himself back onto me. I began to move. Small, gentle in-out, just using the slightest sway of my hips, waiting for him to catch the rhythm. He hardened in my hand, and I increased my speed, feeling him push back against me. He put his hand over the one I had around his dick, my other holding his shoulder. I leaned forward, my chest to his back, reaching to try and kiss his neck, but couldn't. I nuzzled his shoulder blade instead. He pumped his hand harder, forcing me to do the same, now buried deep inside him, each forward thrust making him moan under his breath. It felt good in there, like we fit together perfectly. I was really doing this—not a one nighter, but the brink of a real relationship.

I pulled away until I was almost completely out, pushed back in, the moans turning to grunts that got louder as I moved faster, a piston building to full speed. I had to release him so I could get a grip of his hips, circling my thumbs over his ass cheeks, watching his elbow working hard, the muscles all up and down his arm taut against the skin. I was close. He was close. I wasn't sure I could hold on much longer.

I slowed a little and ran my finger up and down his spine. He moved, not me. I resumed, thrusting up on his down beat.

"Oh yeah," he said. "Right there."

I was done for. I entered the build-up, the heat searing through me, ignited by the sound of his pleasure, his fist pumping hard and fast, with me inside him, making this happen. I slammed into him one last time, stayed there, no longer aware of anything other than the glorious sense of release and sparks in the back of my eyes that knocked out half my visual field. I heard him emit a growl, opening my eyes in time to see his load shoot high into the air. I fell back on my heels, and he fell with me, craning his neck to meet my lips with his.

"Wow, do you know how to fuck a guy!"

I laughed, breathless, sweating. It had been embarrassingly short (isn't it always the first time?) but intense, and I found my thoughts wandering back to Calvin and the earth tremor that had accompanied his arrival in my life. We'd had great sex, epic sex that could last for hours, but you know what they say about quality over quantity? If I added up all the sex I'd had with Donny, Cal and anyone else since, it still didn't come close to this.

Adam eased himself off me and we fell onto the bed, side by side, in each other's arms. I wondered if the earth had moved for him too, because mine was tilting right off its axis, all set to roll deep into interstellar space.

Chapter Thirteen

If I'd known living life as an openly gay man was going to involve spending all my time enduring or avoiding interfering, bossy women, I maybe would've thought twice.

OK, maybe not. I was happier and more content than I'd been in a long time, which isn't to say that the path was running true and smooth for Adam and me. When I wasn't fighting with everyone else, I was fighting with him, over his kneejerk reactions to things said or done, his sudden reversals on our plans to go out, his temper tantrums when stuck in traffic, queuing in the bank, having to step around someone holding him up, me spending too long in the bathroom. I soon lost count of the times he pulled the checkout stunt, and had long since given up trying to get him to see how much his attitude pissed people off when they were probably in as much of a rush as he was.

Not that I had any delusions that I was perfect. I was having my fair share of temper tantrums, though I chose to take them out on the Magda gym equipment. I was struggling with the whole relationship thing and for reasons I couldn't yet share with Adam, because I was only just starting to face up to them myself. Still, the make-up sex almost made up for it—Adam might have been living up to the nickname I'd given him in all other respects (not that he knew anything about it), but he was the most patient, understanding, and considerate lover. Even so, I have to admit the constant conflict was getting me down.

First came the battle with Elise to get my stuff. The day after I'd left she changed the locks on the apartment, which I didn't discover until the following weekend, and she wasn't home, she claimed, but I suspected she was sitting inside, laughing at my efforts to break into what was still my apartment. I called her cell.

"Make an appointment through my attorney," she said, and that was the last time she spoke to me. After that it was all yelling. Her attorney—her boss, Rory, of all bloody people—told me that if I wanted access, a witness would need to be present to make sure I didn't try to take anything that wasn't mine. Like I owned anything in that apartment to begin with. Infuriatingly, the insinuation I would actually *steal* only made me more determined to make damned sure I got half of everything, whether I wanted it or not. She wanted the fridge? Fine. I was taking the dishwasher. Keeping the TV, Elise? Sure! Best order your new sofa now, honey, because that baby's mine. As requested, I emailed Rory my list for Elise's approval. He emailed it back—eventually—with half the items crossed through and an instruction that in the interests of avoiding further distress for Elise, pick-up would be during the week, *and* in the daytime. The hell with Elise's distress. I had a job to keep, a new team to manage.

I went over at the weekend to have it out with her, hoping to grab my things while I was there.

"You're not coming in," she shrieked, attempting to slam the door in my face. I blocked it with a well-placed foot, swearing under my breath as my toes were crushed between the door and the frame.

"You can't stop me, Elise," I shouted. I heard the guard lift on a spyhole across the hall.

"I'll call the police!"

To do what? Turn herself in for maiming me for life? I shoved the door. She shoved back.

"The fuck you are." I shoved again. She let go, sending me hurtling, head first, into our apartment. I staggered to a stop just before I collided with the closet, funnily enough, because surprise, surprise, who should be sitting on MY sofa, drinking out of MY goddamned coffee mug?

"Hey, Jen," I said, offering up my biggest, bestest smile. I was seething with anger and she knew it. "How are things?" I managed through smiley gritted teeth.

"Oh, just great," she replied, eyes flitting between us warring spouses. "I'll, err, go get those papers you needed," she explained to Elise, set down her drink and scurried past me, coughing nervously as she exited the apartment. The door was wide open, which I thought was probably a good thing. I wasn't sure which of the two of us wanted to kill the other more.

"I told you to go through Rory," Elise said coldly. She turned away and refolded the top two items in the neat pile of laundry next to her.

"I tried that. For some reason he thought it would be acceptable to further inconvenience me by insisting I call during the week."

"And?"

"I'm at work!"

"Being at work didn't stop you from screwing *him*, did it?"

I pride myself on being quite a tough, manly kind of guy, so was more than a little horrified by the high-pitched "ha" of disbelief that came out of my mouth.

"Don't you dare!" Elise started before I got any further. I went on undaunted.

"Don't what? Point out the obvious?"

"There's nothing going on."

"You're kidding me, right? Do you seriously expect me to believe that Jen is here to do what? Offer you moral support, a shoulder to cry on?"

"Believe what you like, Sol. I've done nothing wrong. It was you who cheated, not me."

What I couldn't believe was that she was still denying it. What was the point? I could see Jen's clothes in the laundry pile.

Elise continued, "Every time you were seeing someone, I let it go. You'd come back here, stinking of sex, and you know what? I could take that. It's what I agreed to when I married you, so you could hide the fact you were queer from your prissy boss lady. Even when you turned your back on me in bed."

I don't know whether I was more angry that she was claiming I rejected her, or that she'd called George prissy. Both were lies. Everything coming out of the bitch's mouth was a lie, but I was way past controlling my temper, so I shut up and left. It was that or hit her over the head with something blunt and heavy. Like her wit.

Anyone chancing to look in the car as I drove back to Emerson would've thought I was stark raving mad, muttering to myself, saying all of the things I'd wanted to say to Elise, how I hated the way she shoved her promotion down my throat, how much of a coward she was when it came to standing up to her mother, how stupid she made herself look by lying to me, how I'd got through fucking her by pretending she was someone else—I'm kind of glad I kept that last one to myself, as she'd have thrown it right back.

When I got back to Adam's, he was fresh out the shower. He looked me up and down and frowned in query.

"Where's your stuff?"

"Don't ask," I grunted. I needed to vent my fury. He seemed only too happy to oblige, and we fucked, right there in the hallway, him naked, me with my jeans around my knees. It felt dirty and illicit, with his shoulder slamming into the wall, my belt buckle jingling along to a thrusty rhythm. We'd both tested negative on the full battery of STIs, but it was the first time we'd done it without protection, and as I banged into him, my mother's voice popped into my head, harping on about Rock Hudson and Freddie bloody Mercury. It could've ruined the moment for both of us, but I somehow managed to convey to Adam what my ridiculous giggling fit was about, at which he started up a breathless rendition of the mock opera section of "Bohemian Rhapsody."

"Galileo, Fig…oh fuck, yeah! Yeah, like that. Ugh. Ugh." He was yelling loud enough for half the kids on the block to hear.

"Shut up!" I said, still laughing and covering his mouth with my hand. He bit me! "Oh, you are so gonna get it now." I cranked it up a notch, and it was un-fucking-believable how horny we were. I was grunting, he was shouting, both of us were giggling, right up to the moment of orgasm. Man, I can't tell you how incredible it felt, coming inside him, white hot jets launching from my balls and shooting like a rocket right into his soul, while he redecorated the wall with his own swirly signature.

When we were done cleaning up, he went to throw on a pair of sweatpants, returned to the living room and flopped down on the sofa, slinging an arm around me.

"I'll forgive you for laughing all the way through sex," he said.

"How gracious of you," I replied, leaning in to kiss him. He returned it, then looked at me very seriously.

"On one condition."

"Which is?"

"You start sleeping in the bed with me."

***

Adam didn't work regular hours—in the US sense, as in he had a schedule, but he sometimes taught evening classes—so he made an impulsive, executive decision and called Elise. I wasn't impressed, and told him as much. When I was done shouting, he explained she'd agreed to leave my things in the hallway, and whether I thought it was a good idea or not, he was going to get them. What I actually thought was he'd dialed a wrong number and spoken to someone else, but apparently not, as when I arrived home the next night, the deed had been done. He'd got there to find her waiting, pen at the ready to make an inventory of everything he took. Not one to be so easily slain by bitterly betrayed dragons, Adam cranked up the Ashton charm, even going so far as to share a coffee and a chat, before departing with my pathetic plunder of worldly goods, relatively unscathed. A couple of weeks later, Elise sent a check for my half of the apartment, minus the cost of changing the locks and a complete overhaul of the interior. In other words, not much more than a dime.

In the middle of all this was the call I got from Elise's mother, which went something along these lines:

"Solomon, dear, please tell me it isn't so."

"Uh, could you be more specific, Darla?"

"That you've left Elise."

"Yeah," I pushed out a sigh of mock regret. "I'm afraid it's so."

"But I thought you were happy together. You looked happy together. Your wedding was so beautiful, do you remember? Elise was just like one of your princesses…"

By which she was alluding to those possessed of our sovereign isle, as opposed to me personally. I almost said, "I don't do princesses, Darla," but bit my tongue and let her continue.

"…and I just know she'll change her mind about getting that house in Dorchester. I was only looking the other day, and…"

Ah, the old grandkids chestnut again. From this I deduced that Elise had told her parents I'd left because I wanted to "move to Dorchester" and she didn't, but she *had* told them, whereas my own parents remained blissfully unaware that my marriage was over and I was living with a man I'd known for less than two months. I took the coward's route and sent my mother an email, fully expecting her to call the minute she got it. No such luck. The hours of dread and waiting turned to days, to a week—I was beginning to think my confession had gone astray, or ended up in her junk mail. Time for me to grow a pair.

When we next went grocery shopping, I stuck a bottle of bourbon in the cart. Adam eyed it in puzzlement.

"I'm going to call my mother," I said. He nodded and mouthed an "oh." Back at the apartment, I cracked open the whisky, filled a glass, took a long slug, thought I was going to die. My lungs felt like they were on fire.

"Do you think this is a good idea?" Adam asked, hitting me hard between the shoulder blades with his fist to try and halt the coughing fit. No, it definitely wasn't. I gave up on Dutch courage and postponed making the call for another time, when I was sober, and Adam wasn't around to see me squirm at my mother's distant derision.

"You coming?" Adam asked the following morning. It was Saturday and he was in his running gear.

"Think I'll give it a miss," I said. He raised an eyebrow but made no further comment. Once he'd gone I got my phone and hit "call" before I had second thoughts.

"Hello?" a female voice answered.

Ah. Not who I was expecting, but infinitely preferable.

"Hey, Claire." My little sister. "What are you doing there?"

"Oh, it's you," she said glumly. I tried not to take it to heart. Our parents were very difficult people to love.

"How are things?" I tried.

"Erm, well, they've been better," she responded cagily. "I was summonsed."

That was a typical ploy of my mother's—to guilt her children into visiting, and partly why I'd stayed in the States after college.

"Why?" I knew why, but was hoping to be proved wrong.

"Why d'you think?" Claire hissed.

I didn't know how to respond to that, or even if she was expecting me to.

"Hold on," she said. From her end I heard the muted thuds of feet on carpeted stairs, followed by a door being closed. "You still there?" she asked.

"Yep."

"What were you thinking, Sol?"

I drew breath—pointlessly, as she was far from done.

"An email? Are you out of your mind? She was getting on the next plane over there, do you know that? The only way I stopped her was by promising to talk to you about it, except I didn't have your mobile number, and Elise refused to give it to me. What the hell did you do to her?"

"You mean apart from leaving her for someone else?" I asked sarcastically.

"She hates you. To be quite honest, right now I don't like you very much either."

I could totally understand that. Claire was only two years younger than me, and we were very close. She'd known about my relationship with James. She'd even visited me at uni and met Calvin, verily declaring him to be a "man whore" who wasn't good enough for her brother. When I'd told Mum I was gay and she'd refused to accept it, Claire had been the second wave of reason, not that it made any difference. My mother insisted I'd marry a girl, and I did, completely ignoring Claire's advice. She'd said it would come to this eventually, because running away solved nothing.

After a long silence, I said, "I'm sorry." I meant it with all my heart. I heard my sister's heavy sigh. "I need to talk to her."

"Yes, you do, but she doesn't want to talk to you."

"Fine." I was already adjusting to giving up the fight, but it's not that easy when it's your parents. It didn't matter that she'd rejected me, pushed me into choosing the life she wanted for me. She was still the woman who had brought me into this world, sat up with me through nights of teething, tummy bugs and tonsillitis. She was my mum. I wanted her to know that whatever happened, I loved her.

Claire sighed again. "OK," she said. "Here's what we're going to do."

Hurrah for bossy little sisters. She was back in the game.

She continued: "You're going to hang up and call back in five minutes. I'll try and talk her round."

"Thank you, Claire Bear," I said far too gushily, following it up with a super-soppy, "I love you."

"Yeah, yeah. Love you too. Bye."

She hung up.

I watched the clock, counting seconds in my head to hurry along the minutes, wandered to the kitchen, grabbed some juice and returned to the living room, feeling decidedly wobbly. My legs weren't quite my own and I sat on the floor—nowhere to fall—leaning back against the sofa, phone in one hand, glass in the other. My five minutes were up.

Chapter Fourteen

"Hello?" a female voice answered. The right one this time.

"Hi, Mum," I greeted breezily.

"Solomon," she said in that flat, emotionless tone that meant trouble.

"You got my email?"

"Yes, thank you."

The silence descended. I waited it out as long as I could.

"Um, did you want to talk about it?"

"Not really."

I heard Claire say something in the background. My mother shushed her.

"I'm very disappointed with you, Solomon."

"I know. I'm sorry, Mum."

"I don't agree with your decision."

"My decision?"

"Just because it didn't work out with Elise…"

I pinched the inner corners of my eyes, trying to keep my cool. "Mum, do you remember our conversation before I came over here to study?"

"I can't say that I do," she lied.

"Yeah, you do," I countered.

"You were young and impressionable. You didn't know what you wanted."

"I didn't change just because I grew up."

"You still have the choice."

"No, Mum, I don't."

She stopped arguing. I could hear the quiver in her breath. She was crying.

"Mum, I love you. That's why I tried to make a go of it with Elise, but it's not me."

She sobbed.

"I met someone new."

"A man?" she gasped.

"Yes, a man. His name's Adam." I said this just as he returned from his run. He paused in the doorway. I gave him a quick smile to assure him everything was OK. He nodded and continued on his way to the bathroom.

"What about Elise?" my mother asked, still sniffling.

"Elise is fine."

"And are you sure this is what you want?"

"I'm sure, Mum. Adam makes me happy. Doesn't that count for something?"

"Of course it does! What kind of mother gets in the way of her children's happiness?"

I thought it best not to answer that one.

We got through the rest of the call by chatting banally about work and my father's plans to take early retirement. He worked on a rig in the North Sea, and it was a tough, physical job that saw him away from home for up to three months at a time. Mum said that now he was in his mid-fifties, he could opt to retire on a reduced pension, and his back was causing him problems, so he was giving it serious consideration.

At some point during the conversation, Adam clambered onto the sofa behind me and massaged my shoulders. My mother didn't ask about him, not once, but she did tell me she loved me before she said goodbye.

It wasn't long after this that the divorce finalized and Elise officially moved her new "roommate" in—did she honestly think anyone was fooled? It was an utterly blatant and pointless lie, but it was no longer my business. We were divorced, and my parents knew the truth. Time to let things settle…or so I thought, until George kicked up a blinding dust storm with a single, off-the-cuff remark.

"When are you guys getting hitched? I've never been to a homosexual wedding."

I was laughing when I told Adam that night. He...well, let's just say he didn't see the funny side.

"I think we should," he said.

"Been there, done that," I responded flippantly.

"But I haven't."

I left the room to get a beer, returning to find him on his knees. I may have further offended him by commenting on his enthusiasm for giving blow jobs, though I didn't realize it at the time. I was flying to L.A. the next morning for an engineering convention. I kissed him and left, believing all was well...

"I'm going to London," he repeated. I'd missed it the first time due to bad cell reception. I was in the departure lounge, waiting to board my flight.

"Why?" I asked, thinking it was college related.

"We're headed in different directions."

Well, yeah! If you're going to London and I'm going to L.A.

"Why didn't you say something before I left?"

"I only just decided."

"When are you going?"

"There's a flight tomorrow."

Captain Impatient strikes again.

"Can it wait till I get back?"

"What's the point?"

"The point is..."

He'd thrown me. Sure, our relationship wasn't the easiest ride, but I didn't think it was bad enough for either of us to consider fleeing. Not yet. However, if he was asking that question, then clearly he felt something wasn't right. I needed to think quickly. They were getting ready to open the gate and Adam would be gone before I got back. We hadn't been together long enough to survive going "on a break."

"I'll come with you," I said.

What? Where did that come from?

He didn't answer me, but I'd said it, so I'd committed to it. "I've got some leave due. We could make a holiday of it."

Still nothing.

"At least wait for me to get back so we can discuss it?"

"Fine."

Well that was something. The gate opened.

"I'll call you when I get to L.A. Bye."

I hung up, no time to wait and see if he had anything else to say, like those three little words, for instance, not that I'd said them to him at any point. I was still trying to deal with living with a guy, and it was amazing in so many ways that I couldn't begin to explain. But it was also hugely new and disorienting. The good: we liked the same things—running, working out, our jobs, beer, music, funny movies, clutter-free apartments. The sex was incredible, mostly. We still had a few issues to iron out in that regard, like that I was still spending most nights on the couch. The bad: Adam's impulsive decisions drove me to distraction, but I could hardly fault him for that when I'd known it from the start. In fact, we probably wouldn't have been together at all if he wasn't so damned impatient. It forced me to take action quickly, often without the luxury of thinking it through, just to avoid him going off in a huff.

Oh, and according to him I was dismissive.

Yeah, whatever.

Joking aside, it was a defense mechanism. In all of my thirty-one years, I had never felt so connected to another person, so… dependent. I guess that was the part I was struggling with most, and maybe it was a gender thing. Strong and independent woman that Elise was, she still deferred to my maleness within the confines of our relationship. Spider in the bathroom? Sol the spider catcher at your service. Light bulb needs changing? Call Sol for all your electrical needs. If I'd let him, Adam would have taken on all of those "masculine" duties within our relationship in a heartbeat—not intentionally to secure his dominance. It was just the way he was, and the way I was too. To maintain the status quo, I had my own mental list, and it needed to balance perfectly. If he took out the trash, I washed the car. If I made dinner, he did the laundry. I was aware that it was more than a bit nuts, and that I needed to deal with the root cause, if only I could figure out what that was.

***

I arrived back from L.A., fully expecting to find Adam sitting on our packed cases in the hall, and waving airline tickets at me. Actually, I wouldn't have been at all surprised to find he'd already gone ahead of me. That, alas, was not what I came home to.

Adam stood before me, unshaven, his hair all over the place, crumpled clothes, bare feet. His musk reached me a second later. Musk, and alcohol. He stepped aside to let me pass. The place was a mess. Takeout cartons, the bourbon bottle, along with several others, scattered around the floor, empty and lidless.

"What the hell, Adam?" I was shocked. Truly. He stooped to remove some of the clutter, clearing a seat for me on the sofa. I didn't take him up on his invitation, instead helping him clear away the evidence of his week of drunken abandon. He took the trash out, and I opened the window, the hot wind rushing through the apartment, lifting the papers from the desk and depositing them on the floor. I pulled the window almost shut, leaving a two-inch gap to try and vent the stench of stale alcohol, set his papers straight, and waited for him to return.

"I'm going to take a shower," he said, walking right past without so much as a glance my way. I heard the running water, went to make coffee for us both, and resumed waiting.

Still unshaven, he emerged from the bathroom. He took the coffee cup from me with no more than a mumbled thanks. I followed him back to the living room.

"Has something happened?" It was the only way I could think to ask that didn't sound egotistical. Part of his role at the college was to be on the rotating schedule to deal with emergencies, and students could be an anxious bunch, so it might not have been anything I'd done.

"Ha. Yeah, you could say that." His voice was humorless, tired. His eyes met mine for a second. "You happened."

OK. Not egotistical then. So what was this? Second thoughts about our relationship? He'd done all the chasing, not that I'd tried too hard to get away, but it was typical Adam; jump first, look back later to see what it was you landed in.

"You want to be more specific?" I asked.

"Not really." He got up and walked to the window, staring out across campus. It wasn't that great a view, but I gave him a minute or two to admire it before I pressed for more information.

"So what's changed?"

"Nothing." He turned to look at me and shrugged. "It was naïve of me to think that it would."

"I don't get you."

"That you'd change your mind about us."

Confused? You could say that.

I said, hoping it would offer assurance, "I still feel the same about you—us."

He nodded ruefully. "That's what I mean."

We had to be talking at cross purposes. Personally, I'd have been delighted to know someone felt for me the way I felt for Adam. I may not have told him, used the exact words, but I was crazy about him. Surely my offer of taking the trip to London should have left him in no doubt?

"Did you book the airline tickets?"

He shook his head.

"Why not?"

"Because I was leaving you."

And that was when it hit me. Hard. My stomach churned, sucker-punched by the realization of what I'd done. How had I not seen it before? Adam wanted us to get married. He'd even done the whole getting down on bended knee thing. My response? Make a joke out of it and jet off to L.A., which sent out the exact opposite message to "I'm crazy about you." I couldn't believe I'd been so stupid. No wonder he was a mess. But there was a hope in that, surely? His head was screwed because of me, because he thought I didn't care. We could still fix this. Couldn't we?

I got up and walked toward him, thinking on my feet, trying to come up with a way to convince him how much he meant to me. But I was no good at this. He was the impulsive one, whereas I needed time to think, to plan and consider what I wanted to say. He did open and emotional. I did technical, practical, sensible. Straight-to-the-point, no-nonsense communicating came with the territory of being an engineer. However, there was a world of difference between yelling "Stop the production line!" across a workshop, and uttering the words "I need you. Please don't go" to the man standing before me now, miserable and defeated. Because of me.

"Are you still going to leave me?" I asked.

"I don't know." He stepped away, avoiding my gaze. "I'm going for a run."

I watched in a daze as he went to put on his running gear, heard the door close and the sound of his feet against the loose gravel, fading into the distance. I was tired from my trip, and I desperately needed sleep, but I couldn't leave it, not knowing him the way I did.

The way I did? Was three months long enough to get to know someone? Really get inside their head, understand how they tick? Was it long enough to fight for?

I knew he'd have it all worked out by the time he got back, made up his mind based on the facts as he saw them. And the facts as he saw them were what? That we had no future?

With much effort, I got my legs to work, left the apartment, and jogged in the direction of the common.

The wind had dropped, and it was humid and stuffy, the air hanging damp around me, making me feel groggy and grimy. I crossed the street, pausing to peer along the path that cut through the grass and trees, and saw Adam run past the far end, his expression fixed straight ahead. I turned left, so I could intercept his circuit, his decision-making. It was a struggle drawing enough oxygen, and I was feeling breathless as I rounded the edge of the common, anticipating that I would soon see him heading my way. I waited. I waited some more. Five minutes passed by, still no sign of him, which meant he'd either doubled back on himself or veered off somewhere, which was unusual. For some reason we always took the path counter-clockwise, and if we wanted to run longer we carried on in that direction. We didn't double back, and we didn't take shortcuts, but whatever, I now had no idea where he was, and time was running out.

I jogged back the way I'd just come, slowing to a stroll as I approached the exit, a cold sweat descending over me, the outer edges of my vision blurring, tunneling my attention, refusing to let me look away. For there, with his hand on another guy's shoulder, was Adam.

Chapter Fifteen

I don't recall getting back to the apartment, or how long I'd been sitting waiting, but it was dark by the time Adam got home. I had my back to the door, and I heard him stop. If he was watching me, all he'd have been able to see was my outline in the twilight of the evening spilling through the window.

"Sol?"

"Hm?"

"You OK?"

I closed my eyes and stayed completely still. I could have fed him the lie we feed strangers—hey, yeah, I'm fine, thanks—because that's what he felt like to me at that moment. A stranger. I could have got angry, but what good would it do? He'd said he was thinking of leaving me, and I'd still gone to L.A. I had no right to feel betrayed. In his mind I'd already made the decision, and this was his place. It would be me leaving, not him, to go where? Back to the Best Western with my life in a suitcase?

"I'm going to switch the light on," he said. The warning registered a second after the event and I instinctively screwed up my eyes. When I found I could open them without my eyeballs turning to dust, Adam was kneeling in front of me, his head bowed, long dark lashes fluttering against his cheeks.

"I went to find you," I admitted.

"Yeah. I saw you."

"Who is he?"

He closed his eyes, his head shaking from side to side, a slight, rapid motion of denial. Or was it guilt?

"I could tell you knew each other. Were you screwing him while I was in L.A.?"

Back in the days of arguing with Elise, we'd reach that stage of the fight where I'd stop trying to defend myself. If we'd been dueling to the death, she'd have had me face down in the dirt before I'd even reached for my pistol. And she'd yell, "The right to remain silent has no jurisdiction here." And I'd think *Fuck you, Elise*, but I knew better than to say it out loud. Now it was me on the receiving end of the silent treatment, I could appreciate just how disempowering it was. If I'd had the energy to scream and shout I would have done, but I was too tired and couldn't see the point. Not if he'd cheated on me. I sat forward, all set to go and pack my bags and leave.

"Doctor Michael Finnegan," Adam said.

I stayed where I was. He glanced up at me. I was sure I knew that name from somewhere.

"My ex."

Ah, maybe that was it, though I couldn't recall Adam mentioning him by name before.

"He was out for a stroll. He's a bit weird like that. He got dumped and was feeling miserable. After you walked off, we went for a coffee, and I told him all about you."

A smile broke across Adam's face, lifting it with joy. My heart skipped a beat at the realization it was for me.

"Michael said I was to pass on his condolences to you, for having to put up with me, and to look him up if you ever need a sympathetic ear."

I laughed quietly. "You're not that bad."

"I can be. I know I take things too fast for you. I forget how little time we've been together, because it feels like forever."

"It's like that for me too." I shuffled forward, lifting his chin with my finger so I could look into those beautiful quicksilver eyes. "I don't want to lose you, Adam." He leaned his head to the side, my palm now cupping his cheek. It felt so right to be with him. "I thought you were with someone, you know. Back at the checkout?"

Adam frowned. "Why did you think that?"

"You took a call, and it sounded…I don't know. Well anyway, I was jealous as hell."

He thought for a moment and shrugged. "I don't recall, but I wasn't seeing anyone."

"I guess it doesn't matter then." I watched his face for any indication that he might be lying. He stared right back at me, his expression sincere. I smiled. "I bet you can't remember what you said on our first date either."

"What did I say?" The corner of his mouth twitched. He remembered, all right.

"That you were the love of my life."

He smiled coyly. "Yeah."

"I think you might be right."

"Uh huh?"

"Uh huh," I repeated. I took a deep breath and looked away, preparing to say words that were so out of character they didn't even sound like me in my head. I resumed eye contact; held it. "I've never felt like this about anyone before."

"So why do you push me away?"

"I don't mean to. It's just all so new, different. Sometimes I can't deal with how intense it is. And you scare me."

He looked horrified.

"Not like that," I amended quickly. Since that first night, when I'd panicked and fled, he'd remained convinced that I'd been in an abusive relationship, and I have to say, faced with the same evidence I'd think that too. But it wasn't so. I could look after myself. I'd always made sure of that, since James was beaten to death. With much effort, I refocused on the present, meeting Adam's worried gaze.

"How do I scare you?" he asked.

"Just your impulsiveness. I never know what you're going to do from one minute to the next. Like when you left this afternoon? I was so frightened if I didn't find you quickly enough you'd have made the decision to leave."

I saw pain on his face, the reflection of my own. He lifted his hand and pressed my palm to his lips, kissing it once. He shook his head.

"I'm not going anywhere." Slowly he rose to his feet, jiggled one leg and then the other to thwart pins and needles, and held out his hands to me. I took them and he pulled me into his arms. "I missed you," he said.

"I missed you too."

"What I said before you left, about getting married? I meant it. I do think we should, but when you're ready."

I nodded. "What happened to not being the committing type?"

"You were still with Elise. I was trying to offer you a no-strings package."

A no-strings package. Huh.

"I like the package just as it comes, thanks," I teased. Adam smiled and kissed me, the lightest touch of his lips to mine.

"Say the word, and I'll propose properly."

"How will I know you're not just after getting your mouth around my dick?"

"I can do that while I'm down there, if you like."

I laughed. "Gee, you're so romantic!"

"Yep. Like I said, I'm the love of your life."

My mind did a quick scan of the facts, bringing up records for my review. Before Adam, I could honestly say that the only ones who'd really meant anything to me were Elise and James. There he was again, and that gut-wrenching pain that went with the memory of him. Adam was studying me.

"What's on your mind?"

I blinked to clear a path through the shambles of thoughts and memories. "Someone I need to tell you about."

Adam's shoulders sagged in defeat.

"No. Someone from…my old life."

"You loved him very much," he observed. I nodded, feeling tears spring up from nowhere. I buried my face in his shoulder, trying to pull it back together. I wasn't a crying kind of guy. Really. Reminding myself of that helped get it under control again. I cleared my throat.

"I'm so sorry," I said.

"Don't apologize."

"I feel like I'm betraying you every time I think of him."

"You're allowed to have a life before me, and you loved him. How is that betraying me?"

"Because I love you."

Amazing. We build that phrase up into something so grand and meaningful, spend so much time practicing the announcement, that when it comes to the crunch it's almost impossible to push out the words. And it had fallen right out of my mouth, just like that.

Adam put his arms right around me and squeezed until I had to flex my shoulders to stop him from crushing me.

"Ow! What's that for?"

"I've been holding off saying it, in case it was too soon."

I moved back so I could look at him. "It's not too soon."

"In that case, I love you, handsome."

I felt myself grinning, a big stupid grin.

"So that means—" Adam tapped his finger against his lips and studied the ceiling, hamming up thinking about it. "I'm actually the love of your *new* life."

I shoved him away. "You can be such an ass sometimes."

***

We went to bed together—so far so good. Oh, all right, I'd only made it as far as sitting on the edge of the mattress, where I was taking great care to ensure my phone was set to silent. From behind me came a cough to draw my attention. Nothing else to delay, I shuffled down under the covers, cuddled up, felt him harden against my thigh, and made a mental note to make it up to him, because right at that moment I had nothing to offer in return. He held me tight, his fingers firmly locked together so that his arms formed a complete loop around me, presumably so I couldn't run away again. Silly as I felt, I was quite sure if he released me that's exactly what I'd do. No words passed between us in that amber-lit peace, yet I sensed him waiting. Quietly, *patiently* waiting, for the explanation I'd promised him back at the start of this fast and furious love affair of ours.

And so I began to recount my relationship with James, how he'd been killed while I was away at university, that I'd returned home for his funeral. I kept everything simple and factual, because I couldn't say out loud how it made me feel. Not yet. Adam asked for no more than I gave—I was so grateful for that—and for a long time after, we lay there, just holding each other, kissing occasionally. I was so tired, but sleep eluded me. At three a.m. Adam rolled onto his side to face me.

"Is this about James too?" he asked.

That was it. The dam broke, a tsunami of grief surging from me, unrelenting, swell upon swell, engulfing my every shoreline, obliterating my carefully constructed defenses, until all that was left was an ocean of nothing, and in the middle of all that blackness was me, treading water, exhausted, clinging to a fragile life raft, a remnant of the past. I cried till my throat was raw from trying to swallow the memory of the last time I broke down, almost eleven years ago. I'd been through some crap, with Donny, with Cal, and more recently with Elise, but none of them had brought me to this. Not even when I thought Cal had broken my heart, which he hadn't. It was already broken.

Adam was right. He was the love of my *new* life, a lighthouse I had seen in the distance, the place I needed to get to, to start over, begin again.

Chapter Sixteen

"Did they go to prison?"

Our plane lurched to a stop. The safety belt lights went off. I unclipped myself, delaying answering the question Adam had wanted to ask since I told him about James.

"No."

I got up and retrieved my jacket from the overhead compartment. Adam did the same.

"They were never identified," I said, keeping my eyes averted.

"But you know who they are." It was a statement, and a correct one at that. I turned and looked him in the eye.

"It's ancient history."

***

The English late spring air was the purest tonic, filtering through my lungs, into my blood stream, replenishing, oxygenating, invigorating. We rented a car from Heathrow, cleared the M25 and were soon on our way up the A12 to Norfolk, to visit Adam's family. Two weeks in the UK, the second of which would be spent with my parents, but was I going to let it get me down?

OK, maybe I was a little. I was dreading it, to tell the truth, but it was still a week away, so I pushed it to the back of my mind. I was really looking forward to meeting Adam's mum and dad, and his kid brother and sister, not that he'd told me much about them, other than that they were pretty laidback and were eager to meet me too.

It was early evening by the time we turned off the main road and headed cross-country, weaving our way along winding lanes, slowing to pass through villages consisting of little more than a couple of houses and a pub. Having grown up in the Yorkshire dales, I was well used to driving roads like these, except I wasn't the one doing the driving, and Adam had only visited twice since his parents moved from the city to "the sticks." Needless to say, I was playing the backseat driver role to perfection, ordering him to brake when he was, allegedly, already braking, pointing out hazards he claimed he'd already seen, and pre-empting the GPS.

"Would you please shut the fuck up!" Adam growled, taking a bend like a left elbow at forty.

"Only if you slow the fuck down," I snarled back. He slammed on the brakes, throwing me forward violently, pulled into a turning point and got out.

"There! It's all yours," he said, yanking the passenger door open and storming off along the scrub at the side of the narrow road. He stopped, unzipped his jeans, took a piss. I got out and climbed in the driver's seat. He returned, glowering, saying not a word. Seatbelts fastened, we set off again. I doubt we'd even covered as much as five miles when he started fidgeting. I ignored it, focusing on the stuffy English voice of the GPS as "she" commanded, "At the roundabout, take the third exit." I signaled right, entered the roundabout and passed the first exit. Adam reached across and flicked the indicator arm. I flicked it back again and completed a full circuit of the roundabout, sailing right past our exit. Petty? You bet!

Next time around I continued on our route as directed by heavenly bodies, the screen showing we had just three miles to go. Two miles. One mile.

"Your destination is on the left."

I peered across the empty field, aware of Adam's smug expression in my peripheral vision.

"What?" I asked.

He shrugged.

"They live in a field?"

"Nope." He laughed. Bastard.

I peered at the tiny display, trying to make sense of the road layout displayed there, comparing it to the view through the windshield. It kind of looked the same, other than there being a whole lot more houses than on the map.

"Try the next right," Adam suggested helpfully, with a light sprinkling of know-it-all. I did so, and almost grounded the car as it dove into a crater-sized hole in the road. We powered on through, rising out the other side, the new houses still on our right, up ahead of us a big old farmhouse.

"You have reached your destination," quoth she-in-the-box on the dash.

"Have we?" I asked—not her. Adam.

"Yep."

He unclipped his seatbelt, waited for the car to stop and leaned over to kiss me. He grinned.

"Sorry," he said, "but you were being such a pain in the arse."

"Me? Are you kidding?"

He shut me up with another kiss, just as a woman emerged from the gate of the ancient farmhouse. At least I assumed it was a woman, but I was suddenly blinded by a flashlight of about a thousand watts beaming into the car.

"Who's that?" a voice called from Somewhere Beyond. "Who goes there?"

Speaking out the side of my mouth, I said, "You did tell them we were coming, didn't you?"

"I did, yeah," Adam confirmed. He slung open the door, almost hitting the woman with it. "Lay off, Mum," he said.

I watched, or attempted to through my scorched eyeballs, as they embraced each other in a tight bear hug. Their conversation was mumbled, as if I wasn't supposed to be able to hear it.

"You got yourself a real hottie there," Adam's mum said. Her New Zealand accent was incredibly strong.

"You know mums aren't supposed to say things like that?"

"I've got eyes, haven't I?" She released him and waddled around to meet me as I got out of the car. She was a big woman—large breasts, wide hips, tall, curvy and beautiful.

"You must be Solly," she said, extending her hand and using first contact to haul me in for one of those bone-crusher hugs, squeezing the breath right out of me, meaning I didn't get to protest that, with the exception of my mother, sister and James, people usually called me Sol. She released me—almost—grabbing Adam's arm with her free hand and leading us toward the house.

"I'm Maddy, by the way," she explained to me, then to Adam, "Dad's at the pub."

"Great," he said dryly, with a doleful glance my way.

"I'm bloody not!" a voice hollered from behind us. I turned, saw a hefty, dark-skinned man storming in our direction. He walked right up to me and slapped me hard on the back. I just about held my ground. "Warren," he said. "Good to meet you, mate." That enormous hand came swooping down in front of me, gripped my own lesser hand and near shook my arm out of its socket.

"Sol, and likewise," I managed to utter. Warren released me, turning his attention on Adam. The man oozed testosterone. Like father, like…

"Son," he said, throwing his arms around him in much the same way Maddy had done. I watched, completely enthralled by the whole display. Adam's parents were both huge, towering over the pair of us, and at six one and six two we weren't exactly shortstops. Before I knew it, I was being carried to the house by the force of Maddy's grip around my arm, soon thereafter getting ambushed, first by an enormous German Shepherd who answered to both Suky and "noisy bitch," and then by Noah and Lily, Adam's younger brother and sister. Noah was eighteen, the same build as Adam, but looked nothing like him; Lily was the image of him, though a good six inches shorter.

There again, she was only fourteen. She'd probably be six foot ten before she was done.

"A stubby, mate?" Warren thrust a small green bottle of beer into my hand.

"Err, yeah. Thanks."

"So you're Adam's boyfriend?" Lily asked. She sat on my knee!

"That's right," I confirmed.

"Cool," she said.

Yeah, I'd have to agree.

"Noah's gay too," she declared.

Noah turned red. I gave him a quick smile of understanding.

"Do you think it runs in families?" That was Lily again.

I shrugged.

"Give it a rest, love," Maddy appealed on my behalf. I peered through the gathered crowd of Ashtons assorted to watch Adam on his hands and knees, with Suky pouncing at him and tearing around in circles. He glanced up at me and smiled.

Only then did it dawn on me that these crazy people were my in-laws.

My in-laws.

Totally never saw that coming.

***

I awoke the next morning to discover I couldn't move my arms. I lifted my head to try and establish the cause of my immobility, getting a large slobbery lick on the chops for my troubles.

"Hey, Suky," I said. She crawled even further up the bed and batted at Adam with a big heavy paw until he awoke. He rolled over to face me, the dog giving his face a good wash.

"Good morning." His voice was husky with sleep, and he was smiling. Wow, this felt so incredible, other than the large, hairy prophylactic coming between us.

"Off you get, Suke," Adam said. She wasn't happy about it, but she did as he told her. Adam scooted closer, wriggling until his morning wood made contact with mine.

"Cute name for a massive, scary dog," I remarked, my hips starting to move all by themselves.

"Scary? She's a big softy."

I heard her grumble and peered over Adam, laughing at the sight of that big nose resting on the edge of the bed, huge brown eyes staring up at me. She let out a heavy breath that sounded like a sigh.

"I feel guilty now," I said.

"Don't. It's all a cunning ploy for sympathy." Adam put his arms around me and pulled me on top of him.

"Are we really going to do this in your parents' house?" I asked. And of course I was resisting his moves. Hm—true for about three seconds. I lowered my lips to his.

"Thick walls," he murmured. We settled into a gentle rocking rhythm, sliding together easily. He smelled so good I could've got off on that alone, but if we came like this we were going to have some serious cleaning up to do. With difficulty, I moved away. Adam groaned.

"Don't go."

"I'm not." I shuffled on my knees and lay down again, next to him, but facing the opposite way.

"Ah," he said, figuring what I was up to. He moved down the bed to give me legroom, his big hot hands on my ass. I smiled, my teeth touching the head of his dick at the same time as the heat wrapped around mine. I mimicked his movements, circling my tongue around the drawn foreskin, closing my lips around the head, poking the tip of my tongue into the slit. He tasted fantastic—salty, metallic, familiar. He took me deeper into his mouth. I did the same. He sucked. I sucked. I started swaying, pushing deeper still. He matched my moves, grunting approvingly as I rested one hand on his buttock, while the other fondled his balls. His hands roamed, found my hole, a place he had yet to visit. I lifted my topmost leg to grant him access. He wet his fingers and slowly worked his way in, taking great care not to push me, though I was kind of past caring, with his dick filling my mouth, mine filling his. I found myself torn between the two sensations, but as I thrust forward he stayed with me, working me expertly with the tip of his finger. I heard a low guttural groan, realized it was coming from me, and tried to pull back to warn him of the imminent explosion, my grip tightening on his balls as the sensation soared through me, taking me over. I fought to keep my lips closed around him, needing this to be as good for him as it was for me. He increased his tempo, the first spurt hitting the back of my throat, subsequent ones not quite so powerful, pooling on my tongue. I swallowed and kept him in my mouth, gently easing back, still reveling in the taste of him.

He released me, and I somehow crawled back up the bed to join him. We shared the deepest kiss, the lingering taste of ourselves on each other, mingling, merging into one. It was glorious, and wonderful, and I loved him.

I really did. I loved my Captain Impatient.

***

"Laidback" turned out to be something of an understatement. When we finally made it downstairs just before midday, with Suky racing ahead of us and barking excitedly, it was to a kitchen full of Ashtons, eating toast, slurping tea and reading various publications. Lily was scrolling through social network stuff on her phone. Noah was reading a real book—for college, he said, though it looked a lot like trashy fiction to me. Across the farmhouse kitchen table, Warren and Maddy were sharing a disheveled heap of Sunday newspapers.

"G'day," Maddy greeted us. She got up and gave us each a kiss on the cheek. "You boys want some brekkie?"

"Please, Mum," Adam said.

Boys. That amused me. Adam noticed me smiling and gave me a puzzled look. In daylight, Maddy didn't look much older than we were and possibly would have appreciated the compliment of my saying so, but I was treading carefully, trying to make a good impression. Until that point, Lily hadn't noticed us, and when she did, she bounded to her feet, hugging me tightly around the middle. Adam tutted.

"Get off, you," he said, nudging her playfully. She released me and grinned.

"If you ever change your mind about being—"

"Delilah!" Warren cut her off without lifting his eyes from the paper. Sulkily, Lily returned to her seat. I had wondered about her name—guess Mr. and Mrs. A. had a thing for the Old Testament.

"Sit down. You're making the place look untidy," Maddy said, pulling out a chair for me and removing the clean but unfolded laundry from it. Adam was left to fend for himself. He and Noah exchanged a look. I tried not to laugh. The place *was* untidy, but it was…charming. I couldn't believe I'd thought it, but there was no other word. My family was nothing like Adam's, with their hugs and kisses, and their old house full of clutter. I liked it. A lot.

Maddy brought across a plate stacked high with thick-cut buttered toast, placing it in front of us. Oh well, I thought. I suppose a few days of carbs wouldn't matter that much.

"Tuck in," she encouraged. I lifted the top slice from the pile and took a big bite. Melted butter ran down my chin. I think I maybe melted a little too. It was divine. Adam was watching me. He licked his lips, and I blushed.

"Yip," Warren said with a sigh, still reading the paper. I wiped the butter from my chin, taking a moment to observe him. I could see where Adam's coloring came from: his father was very dark, with a broad nose and thick lips. I guessed he was part Māori. He folded the paper and sat back, resting his big hands on his chunky denim-clad thighs. "Lily, go and sort the chooks, will ya, darlin'?"

"Why me?"

"I did them yesterday," Noah remarked pointedly.

"Yeah, but Adam's here now. He could do them."

"Do as you're told," Warren scolded lightly, his tone still peaceable.

"It's OK. I'll do it," Adam said. "I wanted to show Sol around after breakfast anyway."

"Your call, son." Warren got up, pausing to kiss his wife on his way past.

"Chooks?" I asked.

"Chickens," Adam explained. I nodded in understanding. Why wouldn't they have chickens? They lived in a farmhouse.

I finished off my fourth round of toast and decided to leave it at that, completely stuffed and feeling like a million bucks. I picked up the empty cups and plate to take them to the sink, but Maddy shooed me away, so I followed Adam outside, leaving Lily to help her mother. Noah had departed a few minutes before and was standing in the middle of the yard, talking on his phone, chickens everywhere, pecking at the ground and strutting their stuff. A cockerel preened himself on top of the gatepost. Noah gave us a nervous smile and walked off into the expanse of long grass running alongside the house. Adam beckoned to me, and we stepped inside the hot, stinky hen coup, where two birds sat, one up, one down, on the hay-littered shelves running the length of one wall.

"What does sorting the chooks involve, exactly?" I asked.

"Collecting the eggs, a quick disinfect, and throw some corn around."

"Sounds easy enough." I peered up and along the top shelf, where a white hen roosted alone. I think she was watching me.

"Be careful with Betty." Adam nodded at the white hen. "She's a bit narky."

Narky. I hadn't heard that word in a long time. I heeded his warning and took the box he offered, leaving him to brush and disinfect the concrete floor, while I set about collecting the eggs. I started at the opposite end of the shelf to Betty, gently lifting each of the warm, shitty eggs and setting them in the box. As I moved along, Betty clucked and fussed, the volume and frequency of her *puck-puck* rising the nearer I got. There were just two eggs left, right next to her. I edged closer. She clucked. I slid my hand along the shelf, secured the first egg, put it in the box. Feeling brave, I reached for the second egg. Betty pecked me sharply on the back of the hand, drawing blood.

"Fuck!" I said, quickly withdrawing. Betty fluttered her feathers and settled down again. Can chooks be smug? Because she was certainly looking pretty bloody smug to me. Adam was laughing hard, and I had to admit it was kind of funny, even if I was bleeding.

"I should've made you do it," I said. "I mean, you had Elise eating out of your hand."

"I wouldn't go that far," he objected humbly, but it was the truth. He was a charmer, and I was completely under his spell.

After we'd finished with the chooks, we left the eggs with Adam's mum and headed out across the fields with Suky, Adam giving me a brief history of his family's present home as we walked. The farmhouse, yard and meadow were once part of a large farm, the surrounding land bought and filled with new houses long before the Ashtons moved there. The house had been built in the 1700s and was a grade II listed building, although only the chimney stack and the north-facing wall of the original house remained. The rest had been rebuilt and extended at various times in the interceding centuries, making for a unique and strangely beautiful property that would have given my ex-mother-in-law spasms.

We walked for a couple of hours, along footpaths, over stiles, through fields of cattle and sheep, pausing to watch a narrowboat pass by on the Norfolk Broads. I'd never seen them before, and this was a vast waterway, nothing like the narrow, meandering canal that ran near my hometown.

On the way back, Adam pre-empted my question about Maddy being very young-looking.

"Mum was only sixteen when she had me," he explained. "Dad's fifteen years older. They ran away to London when Mum was pregnant."

"Wow. That was brave."

"Yeah. They didn't have visas."

"Illegal immigrants?"

Adam grimaced.

"They've got citizenship now, though, I take it?"

Adam grimaced some more.

"Oh."

"Hm," he said. "They're not married either."

"But he is your biological father?"

"Can't you tell?"

"Well, yeah." I laughed. It was so obvious to look at Adam, with his thick dark hair and sexy olive skin. I tried not to think too hard about it, because that's what was going down. Or, should I say, going up.

"My grandma was Māori," Adam said, dragging me away from the image in my mind of him naked, lying on top of me. I nodded in understanding, and listened as he set off talking about his extended family. I wondered if he'd wanted to tell me about his parents before and felt unable to, because now he was on a roll—man, that voice! His accent was stronger than ever, adding another layer to the rich velvety chocolate—he could've been reading the finance report and I'd have been equally rapt.

We arrived back at the house and ate a Great British Sunday roast, minus the Yorkshire puddings, as we were having chicken, not beef. It was delicious, but I was finding it quite a trial, what with the chooks strutting and pecking just outside the window. After dinner, we went up to our room and napped, because we could, then visited the pub with Warren and Maddy, followed by an early night and more silent sex.

That was pretty much how we spent the week—late breakfasts, long walks with Suky, family dinners, during which Noah hardly said a word, and Lily hardly shut up. She was great fun though, for all that her attentiveness toward me could be inappropriate.

On Friday morning, only Noah was home, and he was surprisingly chatty with no one else around. Adam took Suky for a walk, leaving me to check through my work email, while Noah sat across the table, typing at speed on his laptop. When he reached a pause he sat back and watched me, waiting until I looked up.

"You're not gonna hurt him, are you?" he asked.

"I don't plan to."

Noah correctly interpreted my frown as a sign that I had no idea why he was seeking assurance on his older brother's behalf.

"He didn't tell you about Bobby?"

"No."

"I shouldn't have said anything."

He was right about that, and while I was curious, I could see he felt really uncomfortable about letting the cat part way out of the bag.

"I love Adam. I won't hurt him, I promise."

Noah nodded and gave me a quick, nervous smile. "Thanks. He's a good brother."

"He's a good boyfriend, too."

"Yeah. T-M-I." Noah grinned and for a moment he looked just like Adam. He got up and gave me a playful punch in the arm. "Off to college, see you later."

"See you. Have a good day," I said. I relaxed into the chair, listening to the wind gently rustling the trees, punctuated by the intermittent crow of the rooster standing on the gatepost across the yard. No noise of traffic, air con, people—wonderful, perfect peace. As I watched, Adam came back through the gate, waved to me through the window and smiled that lopsided smile. I was surely in heaven.

***

Our last day with Adam's family: it was raining, on and off, with flashes of bright sunshine between the showers. Warren scowled at the gray sky through the droplet-covered pane.

"Wither's bloody tirrible," he complained. Everyone else nodded in silent agreement, other than me. I thought the "wither" was perfect, considering a few hours from now we'd be trawling up north for a week of torturous hell with my parents—the more drab and dreary the better as far as I was concerned. Claire had promised to come visit at some point, thankfully. She always could stand up to them better than I could.

"Yip," Warren said, followed by the gasped little sigh that was his trademark. "We're going back to Auckland before the winter."

Adam's head slowly rotated until he was looking his father in the eye. His face was a picture, and I was dying to laugh. I guess impulsivity was as much in their genes as their dark, rugged handsomeness.

"Are you serious, Dad?"

Warren didn't answer, but his expression said it all.

"What are you gonna do with this place?"

"Dunno yet."

"I'm not moving to New Zealand," Noah chipped in. "I'm starting uni in September."

"Stay here then," Warren said. He got up and left. That was another of his little foibles. Noah raised his hands in despair.

"Where exactly am I supposed to live?"

"In halls?" Adam suggested.

"I'm only going to Norwich. I was gonna stay here."

"Tough," Maddy told him. "You won't be able to afford the rent on this place."

"Maybe Adam and Sol could come and live here," Lily said.

Adam laughed. "Yeah, right. As if that's gonna happen."

Yeah, right. As if!

But Lily had got me thinking. What if it did happen? OK, engineering jobs in England were few and far between, but I didn't have to work in engineering. Hell, I'd work the local supermarket checkout if it meant being here with Adam, in this big old house. I had to smile at my brain's default choice of a make-do job. Who would've guessed you could find the love of your life, correction, the love of your *new* life, in the checkout line?

See, I was starting to realize that it wasn't really impatience Adam suffered from. In fact, he didn't suffer at all. All those decisions we spend forever agonizing over, only to go and do what we'd have done if it had been a snap decision? Adam, and his parents too, simply cut out the middle man, jumped right in with eyes open and to hell with the consequences. It was very liberating.

"I think we should go for it," I said.

"What?" Adam looked at me in amazement.

"Why not?" I shrugged. "Noah could stay here. You could probably get work at the uni."

"What will you do?"

"Work at Tesco? Tend chooks? I don't care."

"That's, err…" Adam narrowed his eyes. "That's a little impulsive, don't you think?"

"Yip," I said, following it up with one of Warren's little sighs, which made them all laugh.

Adam continued to gaze at me—I chose to interpret it as adoration, though I suspect he was waiting for me to reveal it was all a big joke on him. I kept on smiling. I couldn't help it.

"OK," he said, finally. "Let's do it."

Chapter Seventeen

The minute we walked in the goddamned door. She didn't even wait for it to close.

I won't lie. I was expecting trouble. I gave my mother a kiss on the cheek and a swift, generally insincere, hug. Adam was directly behind me. She eyed him up and down like she was trying to identify his species.

"This is Adam," I introduced.

She nodded curtly, glanced down at our feet, said, "Shoes off, if you wouldn't mind. I've only just had the carpets cleaned." She turned away. "Make sure that door's shut properly, Solomon, please."

Stuffy, English pseudo-middle-class household that ours was, she'd never insisted on the removal of footwear before. She was disarming us, and would no doubt be complaining about the smelly feet next. Adam and I dutifully kicked off our shoes, pairing them neatly against the wall. He rubbed my arm and gave me a wink in reassurance.

"Would you like a coffee?" my mother called from the kitchen.

"Yes, please," I responded.

"That would be lovely, thank you, Mrs. Brooks," said Adam.

"How do you take it?"

"Just milk, thanks."

Silence. We stood in the hallway, not sure what to do.

"Oh, Solomon." My mother's voice was steeped in exasperation. "Take Adam through to the lounge."

I did that. We entered. New suite. Very nice. And clean. Hardly used. Such a stark contrast to Maddy and Warren's place, with its saggy sofa and muddy floors, peeling paintwork, pans hanging from the rafters, chooks…

"Here we are," my mother said, placing the two floral china mugs on silver-plated coasters. When Americans think of "England," this is precisely what they imagine. I swear my mother wasn't as bad when I was younger, though. She left the room again. I realized I'd sighed heavily. Adam took my hand in his.

"It's fine," he assured me. I nodded, perhaps hoping that by agreeing with him it would make it true. My mother returned.

"So, Adam." She perched uneasily on the edge of the armchair, smiled, tried to ignore our hand-holding. And failed. "What is it that you do?"

"I'm a teacher," Adam said.

"Oh." She nodded approvingly. "What do you teach?"

"Performing arts. I teach at Emerson College."

"Not at Harvard University?"

"No. I was offered a position there, but I decided to go with Emerson. I like the atmosphere."

My mother was suitably impressed, as was I. Adam hadn't told me he'd been offered a job at Harvard. There again, I'd never asked.

"Do you work, Mrs. Brooks?" he asked.

"Please, call me Betty."

Adam still had hold of my hand, and he squeezed, really, *really* hard. I probably should've prepared him for that one, but it was too good a comedy opportunity to miss—that my mother shared her name with Psycho Chook.

"Betty," he repeated, with difficulty. I was trying, and only just succeeding, to contain the giggles.

"I don't work, Adam, no. Solomon's father is a senior engineer on one of the biggest oil rigs in the North Sea."

"Oh, right," Adam acknowledged tightly. I could feel the tension running right through him, and it made me worse.

"I'm just…" Helplessly, I pointed at the stairs and made a run for it, clearing them two at a time and leaning back against the bathroom door with my hands over my face, tears streaming from my eyes. Below me the conversation continued. Actually for conversation, read "interrogation," because in a previous existence my mother definitely worked for the Gestapo. I wanted to go and rescue Adam, I really did, but I could not for the life of me get the giggles under control. It was nerves, not that it helped any to recognize why I was tittering like a schoolgirl, though I did manage to pause momentarily at the sound of the doorbell.

"Oh. One moment," my mother said. I listened to her open the door. "I didn't think you were coming until Tuesday."

Hm. Someone she was expecting. I kept listening. The door closed.

"Hi. You must be Adam."

Claire. Thank the Lord for great big and very welcome mercies. I flushed the unused loo and legged it downstairs, slowing as I reached the hallway. Adam was on his feet, smiling and shaking my sister by the hand.

"Claire, I presume?"

"That's right. It's lovely to meet you."

"You too."

"Ahem." That was me. Claire pirouetted to face me.

"Grunty!" she squealed and came running at me. My sister was petite and jumped into my arms, lifting her feet from the floor.

"Hey, you," I said, holding her tight for a moment, and then lowering her back to the ground. "You're looking great."

"Thanks. So are you. I've really missed you."

"I've missed you too. You've met Adam?"

"Oh yeah," she said with a wicked grin. She had her back to the others and mouthed silently at me, "He's gorgeous."

"He is," I agreed. Arm in arm, we rejoined Mum and Adam.

"They've always been just the same," my mother told him, with her gaze on Claire and me. It was true. We'd never fought, not even as kids. Well, there was just the one fight, over me marrying Elise, but that was all done with now. I sat down next to Adam, Claire on my other side, both of them holding my hands. My mother eyed us in disdain. Such terrible, conspiratorial offspring.

"I've put you in your old room, Solomon, and Adam in the spare room."

Claire fielded that one on my behalf.

"Mum! Why have you put them in separate rooms?" Before my mother even drew breath to answer, Claire continued, "You let John share with me."

"Yes, but you're getting married."

"How do you know Solly and Adam aren't getting married?"

"Oh, Claire, don't be pedantic."

"Did you ask them?"

"It's fine," I interjected. I didn't want an argument. "We'll get a room somewhere."

"Where?" My mother's tone was brusque. "This isn't Boston, Solomon."

Yeah, I'd kind of noticed, Mother.

Aside from the lack of hospital, supermarket, sports center and high school, our hometown possessed just one bed and breakfast, predominantly used by the local council for emergency housing, and then there were the rooms over the King's Head pub, an establishment owned by Mr. and Mrs. Coolican, aka mother and father of the late James Coolican, aka my first boyfriend, beaten to death at the tender age of twenty by ignorant bigoted fuckwits while on his way home from a night out with friends. Going to stay at the King's Head was deliberately walking into my own personal hell, but I'd rather take that any day than fight my mother over sharing a room with Adam.

"I'm sorry," she said, "but I…I can't."

For what it was worth, she did sound genuinely sorry. I nodded and smiled sadly.

"I know, Mum."

I just had to keep in perspective that the last time I made her face up to who I was, she'd ranted about Freddie Mercury and AIDS. This time she was meeting me halfway. We were here, and she was making an effort with Adam. So, the only other obstacle now was my father.

"When's Dad home?" I asked.

"Tomorrow."

"OK. We'll go and get booked in somewhere, come back tomorrow."

"Won't you stay for dinner?"

We stayed for dinner. It was…well, it was awkward, to say the least. Adam and Claire chattered like they'd known each other forever, leaving me at my mother's mercy.

"How's Elise?"

"Fine, last time I saw her."

"Is she still a solicitor?"

"Yeah, kinda."

"Oh, Solomon. We use the Queen's English here."

Huh.

"Well, Mother, in the United States of America, one does not refer to those who practice law as solicitors. Indeed, one would imagine that one's ex-wife is in a position akin to that of a barrister in English law."

My mother glared at me. Claire kicked me under the table. Adam fidgeted uncomfortably. I stuffed a large piece of cod fillet in my mouth, swallowed, followed by another, and another, endeavoring to clear my plate as quickly as was possible without choking to death. The food, I'm sure, was delicious, but I couldn't stand being there any longer. When everyone else caught up, Claire and I washed the dishes, returning to the living room, where my mother was once again perched on the chair, telling Adam all about my father's job. I waited for her to finish and nodded at Adam.

"Are you ready?"

"Yeah, sure."

He stood up, as did my mother. As she moved toward the door to see us out, I intercepted and gave her a hug. She looked taken aback—understandably, as I don't think we'd properly hugged since I was about eight years old.

"See you tomorrow," I said. While Adam and my mother shared a clumsy mix of handshake and embrace, I hugged my sister tightly. "In a bit, Claire Bear."

"Laters, Grunty," she said. She gave Adam a big hug.

"Grunty?" he queried.

"It's not a very exciting story." She squeezed his hands and released him, nodding and smiling with that look that is approval and warning all in one. That's my little Claire Bear, always looking out for me.

We said our goodbyes, put our shoes back on—duly noting Claire didn't have to remove hers—and went out to the car.

"Grunty?" Adam asked again once the doors were closed. I waved at my mother and sister. They waved back briefly and returned inside.

"Solomon Grundy," I said.

"Huh?"

"You've not heard the nursery rhyme about Solomon Grundy?"

"Nope. Can't say I have."

"Solomon Grundy, born on a Monday…which I was."

"You were named after a nursery rhyme character?"

"It's no different to you all being named after people in the bible."

"Fair comment."

I was glad he'd agreed. I hated being named after Solomon Grundy. Like tempting fate—died on Saturday, buried on Sunday—kind of put a damper on weekends.

"Well, anyway," I said, concluding the point, "Claire thought it was Solomon Grunty and it stuck."

Adam grinned. "It's a good fit."

"Don't!"

"I mean, you do kind of grunt when we're—"

"Adam, seriously." I was trying to be cross, and failing miserably.

"Don't I get a pet name yet?"

I faced straight ahead.

"It'll make up for you not warning me your mum shares her name with the queen of the roost."

That revived our earlier giggling, and we continued to do so until we neared the King's Head, at which point my stomach landed in my shoes. I pulled into a parking space and stopped the engine.

"You OK?" Adam asked. I nodded and gave him what I hoped was a carefree smile. I could see he didn't believe me. "You've gone a funny color," he observed.

"I'm all right," I said. We got out of the car and went inside. James's mum was behind the bar. I felt like I was going to throw up.

"Hello, stranger!" She greeted me with a big, happy smile.

"Hi, Mrs. Coolican," I replied. It was a major effort to sound casual. She laughed gently.

"Mrs. Coolican? That's very formal. It's Yvonne to you."

Until then I hadn't even known her first name; she was just "James's mum" or "Mrs. Coolican," landlady of the King's Head.

"Are you here on holiday?" she asked.

"We are, although we're thinking of moving back soon."

Interesting. I really didn't know James's mum—Yvonne—that well. Other than his funeral, we'd only ever shared a polite "hello," so quite why I'd told her our plans, when I hadn't so much as mentioned them to Claire or my mother, I had no idea.

"Back here?" Yvonne asked. I could tell by her tone she didn't think it likely.

"Norfolk."

"Oh, right. I was going to say—there's not much of anything here these days." Momentarily her eyes became glassy. She switched back. "All the businesses are moving out—there's only this place, the B and B and the post office left, and they're looking to close that down at some point."

The post office. Lots of happy memories for me there: going with my mum and sister to post letters to my dad out on the rigs. It was how we got through the winter months, when the weather was bad. Sometimes he wouldn't get our letters until he came back to shore on his way home, because the sea was too rough for transport to get out, but we kept writing them anyway. These days Mum stayed in touch with him through email. I hadn't written him in years and the thought made me nostalgic for those trips to the post office, leaving our letters with "Aunty Pam" and then departing with our little paper bags of strawberry laces and jelly teddies.

"That's a shame," I thought aloud. Adam and Yvonne were both frowning at me. "The post office," I explained. Adam tutted.

"Do you want a drink?"

I got the feeling he'd already asked me once. I blushed and turned my attention to the ornate brass handpumps along the edge of the battered oak bar.

"Old Brewery Bitter."

In Norfolk we'd stuck to lager, because Warren had a tab and they kept bringing pints over without us asking. However, like most Yorkshire lads, I was a bitter drinker at heart. There were a few places in Boston that sold a decent passing imitation, but it was never as good as the real thing—that uniquely warming mix of rich, dark molasses and tangy aftertaste of hops, topped by a three-quarter inch head of thick creamy foam.

"Two pints of bitter?" Yvonne confirmed.

"Yeah, thanks," Adam said.

I waited for her to start pulling beer into a glass before I made our next request.

"We also need a room, if you've got any available?"

"We've only got one person in at the moment, so you can take your pick. A twin, is it?"

"Double."

"Oh!" She quickly glossed over her reaction, but Adam had already seen it and was staring away across the pub, avoiding looking at me.

My nausea continued all the way through booking our room and confirming we wanted breakfast—Full English, of course. We retired to the beer garden with our pints of dark ale, both of us silent for a long time. There were quite a few other people sitting at the picnic tables dotted around the walled-off courtyard, and I tuned in to their different conversations, every so often glancing at Adam, deep in thought, spinning his glass between his hands. I had a feeling I knew what was troubling him. I reached across and put my hand on his, granting him permission to speak. He went through a couple of false starts.

"You were in the closet."

"Apart from when I was at uni." I closed my eyes, swallowing back the saliva, still not convinced that I wouldn't throw up all over him. "That was James's mum," I explained.

"The landlady?"

I nodded. I wasn't looking at him, but I knew he was watching me, worrying about me. I glanced up through my eyelashes.

"We could've booked into separate rooms, you know," he said gently, reassuringly.

"No. I've got to deal with this. I've run away from it long enough." I looked up again. There were tears in his eyes.

"You're so brave," he said. "And I feel honored to be with you."

I attempted a smile. "You know, that's kind of mushy?"

He blinked a few times and laughed tearily. "Yeah, it is. You've been through so much to get to this point—your parents, Elise, your job, this small town—I'm beginning to appreciate why you pushed me away. I made it even more difficult for you, and for that I'm sorry."

"Hey! Don't start regretting it."

"I don't regret any of it. I only wish I'd understood better. I would've been more patient."

That made me smile for real. I took out my phone. "Call me."

"Why?"

"Just do it."

"It'll cost us a fortune."

"I don't care. Call me."

He submitted and pulled up my number on his phone. Mine started to vibrate in my palm.

"So, you were wondering about pet names?" I turned the screen toward him. He squinted to read it, looked up at me, back at the screen, and shook his head. I dismissed the call and put my phone away again, let it sink in awhile.

"Patient?"

"Yeah, though I'll admit I had you down as Captain Impatient at the start."

"That'd be right. What made you change it?"

"Because you *are* patient, in the ways that matter."

"Pushing in at the checkout?"

"Doesn't matter."

"Asking you to move in with me after two weeks?"

"Doesn't matter either."

"Hm." He rubbed his chin thoughtfully. He'd shaved before we left the farmhouse, so he was all smart and tidy, set to impress my mother. She was easily swayed by such things. I, on the other hand, was looking at the barely visible shadow on his lip and chin, wishing there was a little more stubble there. I loved the rasping of his whiskers against mine. I shuddered at the thought. It was pure desire running through me. I picked up my pint and downed it in one go.

"I'll get our things from the car," I said. His mouth sloped into a lazy smile. I wanted to kiss it, needed to, in fact, so I did, right there in the beer garden—not a full-on, lingering, tongues an' all kiss, mind you, but still enough to give him a taste of what I had planned. I slowly moved away, noting the flush of color in his cheeks.

"I'll come give you a hand," he said.

We took our empty glasses with us, depositing them on our way through.

***

I'd seen him, sitting in the corner of the beer garden. I couldn't believe he'd stuck around, let alone had the nerve to drink in the King's Head, of all places. I don't suppose he recognized me. I'd changed a lot—grown taller, bulked out, gained a whole truck full of confidence. But I'd seen him watching Adam and me. And I knew what he'd done.

Chapter Eighteen

In the past, like many of the old inns across England, the King's Head Hotel had been a traveler's rest. These days, most were owned by large chains, and while they often kept "hotel" in their name, the rooms upstairs were used to accommodate the pub's managers. The King's Head, by contrast, was still a free house, with two floors above the bar: the first, blocked by a fire door marked "Private," was where the Coolicans resided. Our room was situated on the second. It was basic, but clean and well-decorated, with a small cubicle in the corner: a wetroom like those found in trailers, where the toilet and washbasin are effectively within the shower stall. We were at the back of the building, overlooking the beer garden, the sound of chat and clinking glasses floating up through the open window. The cool breeze picked up the scent of the honeysuckle screen, wafting over me as I waited for Adam to finish showering. The pub was next to the parish church, at the highest point of the town, and from where I was sitting, the view as far as the eye could see was of green hills crisscrossed by drystone walls, and dotted with sheep. It was a beautiful place to visit, not so much to live in. Adam emerged from the "bathroom," and I moved to pass him. He halted me with a hungry kiss, his tongue probing inside my mouth, exploring as if he had never been there before. With difficulty, I pulled away from him.

"Be right back," I said, trailing my hand over the bulge under his towel. I took the quickest shower ever, scrubbing frantically with the facecloth to make sure I was absolutely as clean as I could be for him. He'd waited long enough, and I was ready to let him in.

He lay on the bed, the towel still wrapped around his lower body, still aroused. He watched me approach and reached out to rub his hand over my enduring erection. I could feel the blood pulsing through me, my heart hammering in anticipation. I removed my towel and lay down next to him, leaning over to kiss him, my hand straying down to his nipples. I gently pinched the one closest to me, waited for it to harden, rubbed my fingertip over the nub. I repeated this with the other nipple, slowly trailing my mouth down his chin and neck, running my tongue over the dark chocolate circle, sucking and biting until he gasped. I paused to change position.

"Don't stop," he said breathlessly. I smiled.

"I wasn't going to."

I moved across to the other nipple, my dick now pressed hard against his hip. He pushed one hand down between us to stroke me, the other searching out the lube on the bedside table. He stopped to take the cap off the tube, expecting me to hold out my hand. I shook my head and took the lube from him.

"Are you sure?" he asked. I didn't reply, waiting for him to tell me how he wanted to do this. He shifted across and patted the bed. I went to lie on my front. Adam took one of the pillows and rolled me onto my back.

"Lift up," he said. I did, and he put the pillow under my ass. "We're doing this slowly, OK?"

I nodded, watching him squeeze a huge dollop of lube into his hand. He moved down the bed, leaving a trail of kisses in his wake, stopping to suck me, his arm sliding down between my legs. I bent my knees up and felt the first touch of his hand, smoothing over me, covering me in lube, warm, firm strokes, followed by the gentle prod of a fingertip against my hole.

"Have you ever done this before?" he asked.

"Once."

He pushed gently. I tried to relax, but I felt under pressure. It was of my own making. He eased off, waiting a moment before he pushed again. It felt good, and I started to open up to him. He continued to move carefully in and out, returning his mouth to mine, as always, just what I needed. His kisses seemed to melt my insides, as if nothing in the world could touch me with his breath filling me, sustaining me. It seemed strange to think about love at a time like this. Sure, we all like to believe we do, but when that animalistic instinct takes over, the only thing driving us is the search for release. At that moment I was somewhere between the two states, completely overwhelmed by how much I loved him, that conscious feeling about to be drowned by the arousal building in my groin. I felt more pressure against my sphincter, knew it was a second finger, and focused on the kiss, pushing my tongue into his mouth at the same moment as I accepted him once again. My cock twitched eagerly. My God, I wanted him, but I bowed to his experience, his…*patience.*

The slow build was a heavenly form of torture. Compared to Donny's stark, blunt entrance and the excruciating pain that accompanied it, this was bliss. Adam changed position, crouching over me so that he could still kiss me while working me—with three fingers now. We were nearing the point of being in agreement that I was really ready for him to…

I pushed on his chest to lift him from me so I could speak.

"Before this goes too far, I want you to know I love you."

"You're not going to die, Sol."

I laughed. "I didn't think I would."

He rolled his eyes and resumed fucking me with his fingers for a little while longer. I'd have lubed him up myself but I was barely functioning outside of the sensation of his touch. He withdrew, applied more lube to both of us and lowered himself between my thighs, the smooth head of his dick pressing against me, a slight burn already beginning.

"When I push, you push too."

I looked up at him in horror.

"What if I shit?"

He smiled and kissed me, kind of condescendingly. "You won't," he said.

How to ruin a moment! I wasn't a virgin. I knew about these things. No need to panic.

Adam wrapped his hand around me, tugging me, watching my face.

"Better?" he asked. I nodded and lifted my head to capture his lips. He slowly pushed into me, little by little, pausing each time I held my breath. It was so easy, being together like this. I felt no requirement to be anything but what I was. I felt safe, and loved, and as he broke through that final wall of tension, we both groaned aloud, and then laughed about it. From there on, I was kind of out of it, conscious of nothing, beyond the two of us. I recall feeling so full of him, the thought going around and around my mind that he was inside me. Adam. My captain. Making love to me, slowly, gently at first, but each thrust sent him deeper, made me push back harder. His balls were banging against me, the hairs prickling and tickling, stimulating all of my nerve endings at once. My dick was sandwiched between us and that really was enough. I was so close, trying not to cry out even though I was in the most incredible state of pleasure, and pain. Adam was panting, his breath sending shivers running right through my body. He pushed, I relaxed, he pulled, I squeezed. The bed squeaked, I moaned, he grunted, an erotic percussion with an ever-quickening tempo. He was shaking, right on the edge, and that tipped me over too. I grabbed his face with both hands, pulling his mouth down hard to mine, the kiss muting our cries as we soared together, high into the air and came crashing down to earth again.

He pulled out and I grimaced, a little from the pain, though mostly at the immediate sense of loss. I reminded myself that it was the first, not the last time he would make love to me.

***

"Hey, handsome."

I snuggled down under the duvet, refusing to open my eyes. "Hey, Cap'n."

Adam chuckled and kissed my cheek. "It's almost nine. We're gonna miss breakfast."

"Hm, 'kay." I rolled onto my side, a minor twinge serving to remind me of the night before. Amazing. Donny Dickless left me crippled for days, and while I'd be lying if I said I wasn't suffering a little, my wounds were healing nicely.

"Come on, sleepyhead," Adam goaded, not that he seemed in much of a hurry to get out of the bed either.

"You first," I said. My mind was drifting, half-asleep still. However, some of me was very much alive and kicking. It was a bad idea. But…

"What are you doing?"

I straddled him, sliding back so that I lifted his dick with my crack, and pushed down. I yowled. Definitely a bad idea. I lifted up again to reposition myself. That was better. I started to rock back and forth. Adam watched me with a slight smirk. I must have been making some really funny faces, trying to keep the momentum when my glutes felt like I'd run a marathon. He lifted his head so he could watch the motion of our dicks rubbing together, one of those big, hot hands now coming into play, his fingers wrapping around us both. I stopped rocking, let him do the work, and what short work he made of it. As I came, I inadvertently tensed and it made me swear. I felt Adam lose focus and reached under my balls to grab his, squeezing gently as he thrust up, his come mingling with mine as it ran down his hand. I shifted my gaze to meet his, both of us smiling and probably looking just as goofy as each other. But then I remembered what the day had in store. I got up, drawing breath sharply as I staggered to the shower.

"You don't fancy going for a run then?" Adam called after me.

"Run?" I repeated, sticking my head around the sliding door. "I'm having enough trouble walking!"

"Sorry. I tried to be gentle."

"You were."

I showered quickly, as did Adam, both ready for our breakfast—the smell of frying bacon was drifting up from the kitchen, making our bellies rumble. Other than Yvonne and James's dad (I had a feeling he was also called James—Jimmy), we were the only other people in the pub, which was massive and chilly, citrus furniture polish battling to overthrow the aroma of yesterday's beer. I felt…weird. I tried to pinpoint why and by the time I did, Yvonne was in front of us with two large plates loaded with bacon, eggs, fat herby sausages, black pudding, fried bread, baked beans—it looked superb. She set down the plates on one of the round bar tables, pulling two sets of cutlery from the pocket of her chef's apron.

"There you go, lads. Eat up."

"Thanks, Yvonne," Adam said, his eyes almost the same size as the enormous yellow yolks of the sunnyside-up eggs. Sunnyside up—like we do them any other way in England! Jimmy followed up with a tray containing a little steel teapot, milk jug and two mugs.

"Thanks," I echoed, aware that it didn't sound quite so heartfelt as it was. Still distracted, I sliced the end off a bacon rasher. My appetite was fading. What on earth had possessed me to think staying here was preferable to suffering at my parents' house, when the last time I'd been inside the King's Head was for James's wake? I guess in the end the "where" didn't matter—I was trying to hide from memories stored inside my head by avoiding physical reminders. There was no escape.

"Sol?"

"Hm?"

I looked across the table, saw Adam's nearly empty plate, and glanced back at my own, still full apart from the missing end of bacon.

"Eat," he said.

"Not hungry."

"I know, but you still need to eat."

I sighed, somehow choking down the rest of the rasher of bacon and one sausage without prompting.

"A bit more," he instructed.

I shook my head and put my fork down.

"Don't make me feed you."

"As if you would!"

He picked up my fork, scooped some of the beans.

"Here comes the choo-choo…"

"OK!" I grabbed his hand and the fork, and ate the beans. He did it again, and again. It was starting to annoy me, but then I began to feel a little more like myself. He was right. I just needed food. Low blood sugar and dehydration—Adam passed me a mug of tea.

"Better?" he asked.

"Better," I said.

"You want to talk about it?"

"Not here."

We took our plates to the kitchen door. Yvonne was sitting on a high stool, writing on a thick white pad.

"Everything OK?" she asked.

"Yes, thanks. Delicious."

She observed the half-full plate and gave us that questioning look mothers have.

"That was me," I said apologetically.

"You not well, love?"

"Just tired, I think."

"Oh, heck. Well you take it easy. Got anything nice planned for the day?"

"Going to my parents' later—my dad's coming home."

"I heard he was retiring?"

Did she? From whom?

She looked like she was going to say something else about my parents, but thought better of it. She smiled. "We serve food till nine," she said. "If you don't get round to eating elsewhere."

Well, it was a small town, and everyone stuck their nose into everyone else's business, but my parents weren't *that* bad.

"Actually," Yvonne continued, "you can do me a favor." She slid off her stool, lifted a hardcover book down from the top of the fridge and passed it across. *Song of Solomon*—hilarious—could be any one of a hundred books with that same title. "Tell your Claire I said thanks. I really enjoyed it."

I took the book, holding Yvonne's gaze. *She knew.* I somehow mustered a smile, the fizz of tears rising in my throat. She squeezed my hand and released, glancing past me to Adam. I turned away and followed him, out to the car, fell into the passenger seat. He closed the door. I broke down.

Chapter Nineteen

Adam drove without direction, through winding country lanes, revving to climb hills, braking hard as we swooped down into valleys, keeping his eyes on the road, maintaining a silent vigil, while I wept, so far into my grief that I was past caring how unmanly it was. After however long—I had no idea, actually—Adam slowed, stopping next to a tattered wooden gate set back from the road. He switched off the engine and turned in his seat to face me. I stared out the windshield, across the fields, watching black and white dairy cows make their cumbersome stop-start expedition in search of lusher pasture. I had nothing new to say. I'd told him about James. He would have understood Yvonne's unspoken message as well as I did, so he knew all that I knew. And still I felt like a lead weight was meat-hooked to my soul, ripping and wrenching it down, down, down.

There are always those in our lives we might describe as happy-go-lucky—the sort who take everything in their stride, and could be dragged through hell for all eternity but still keep smiling. Like George. Widowed young, with kids to care for, fighting to keep her house, scrambling her way up the career ladder in a notoriously sexist industry, stamping on the fingers of anyone who dared to try and stop her. She just kept on smiling, and I admired her for that. She was the best boss I'd ever had, my champion. My friend. I, on the other hand, had never been one of those kinds of people, not that I was usually prone to falling apart at nothing more traumatic than an uneaten breakfast. One of my schoolteachers used to call me Solemn Solomon, because I was always so serious. Factual, practical, objective—perfect traits for engineering, and I was quite resilient. So what was this?

Adam reached across and took my hand in his, still without a word. I had sorely misjudged him. So much patience, I felt like I was abusing it with my misery, ruining our trip, when it had been his original intention to go it alone.

Because he was leaving me.

The thought set me off on a new round of tears, and his patience finally started to ebb.

"You said you wanted to talk to me," he said.

"I've told you everything already."

"Then tell me again."

"Where do I start?"

"James. Tell me what he was like."

"He was…" I paused to bring up the image of him in my mind, so I could describe him. I couldn't do it, couldn't find the words to do justice to his memory. I took out my phone and loaded the one and only photo I had of him, from the newspaper report about his death. It was taken a couple of years before the attack, so he must have been about eighteen, gone was the chubby cherub face I had loved to kiss, in its place high cheekbones and a square chin, those blue-sky eyes still sparkling with fun and life. He was a beautiful young man—slim and fair with crazy blond hair that was always too long—it used to fall right down over his eyes and would turn the color of caramel during our sessions under the covers, working up a sweat. I came in his hair once, and it dried in rigid toffee stalactites right across his forehead. We tried rinsing it out, but it didn't work. It was around that time he told his parents he was gay—I never asked him why he'd chosen that particular moment to tell them, terrified that they'd spotted his stiff hair and demanded an explanation. But they hadn't known about us back then, or at his funeral.

Adam handed my phone back. "He looks a bit like Bobby," he said.

"Your brother mentioned him."

"Did he? What did he tell you?"

"Nothing. He wanted to make sure I wasn't going to hurt you, and once he realized I didn't know about him he said no more."

"Oh. Well, there's not much to tell. Bobby and I were roommates at uni, along with a couple of others, but we weren't officially an item. I think he saw me as a back-up for when he didn't have a boyfriend. We got a place together after we graduated, stayed there until he decided I couldn't give him what he needed and moved out."

"When was that?"

"Just before I went to Boston."

"And did he hurt you?"

"He hurt everyone. He had a drug problem, stole stuff from me to pay for it. It reached the point where I had to fit a lock on my room and didn't leave anything where he could get at it. One day he smashed the lock and nicked my laptop. It was brand new and had all of my work on it, my photos, music, everything. He sold it for fifty quid. I told him I was going to leave if he didn't get help. He did a runner, left me with all the rent to pay."

"What a prick."

"Yeah, he was an idiot, and I should've laid down the law a lot sooner, rather than believing I could help him. But I think he finally got his act together. He sent me a message last Christmas, said he'd been through rehab and was sorry for everything. I ignored it, thought it was more of his usual manipulation—that's how he'd get people to lend him money. Then I got a PayPal notification that he'd sent me a thousand pounds. I replied to say thank you. That's the last I heard from him. Nicely deflected, by the way."

I smiled. "Hey, you mentioned Bobby, not me." I unlocked my phone screen to look at James again. "You said I was brave, but I wasn't. I was a coward. He was the brave one." I ran my thumb over the photo. "Look where it got him." I watched until my phone screen dimmed. It was gone midday and we were due at my parents' place. I locked my phone and put it away. "We'd best make a move."

Adam's eyebrow rose.

"What?" I asked.

He shrugged and started the car. As he reversed, he said, "Given that being openly gay got him beaten to death, I'd say you were being cautious, not cowardly."

"Yeah, well, it's not you with blood on your hands."

"It wasn't your fault, Sol."

"I didn't say it was!" I sounded defensive. He let it go.

We must have been driving in circles, because we pulled up outside the house less than fifteen minutes later. My father had yet to arrive, my mother was cleaning, and Claire was about to head out to the supermarket for supplies of the alcoholic variety.

"I'll come with you," I suggested, not wanting to be left alone with my mother. Nor was it my intention to abandon Adam, but that's what he assumed.

"You not coming?" I asked him.

He shrugged. "I didn't think I was invited."

I tutted, making light of his misunderstanding, but it had resonated on a deeper level.

We drove to the closest supermarket, which in the US would've been considered a local store. By UK standards it was "bloody miles away." As we wandered the aisles, Claire gabbled on about her wedding plans, and I was listening, kind of. Oh, who am I kidding? I didn't hear a word. I was watching Adam, the subtle glances my way to see what I thought of it all. I could feel the pressure mounting, building inside with no outlet. I couldn't stand it anymore.

"I'll wait outside," I said, and made a hasty retreat, pausing only for the automatic doors to slowly swish and let me pass. I kept going, right through the car park, right through the pain, the physical reminder of our love-making and the mental torture both lessening the longer I walked. I traversed the perimeter of the car park, trying to get my head together, an increasingly urgent requirement, as I was almost back at the entrance to the store and could see Adam and Claire queuing at the checkout. She was loading stuff onto the belt, still chattering, and Adam was nodding and smiling, occasionally looking past her, searching for me. He found me, smiled and pointed at the space in front of him, a reference to how we met, how long ago now? Not yet four months—just enough time to get a divorce, to form a habit, to make a complete and full recovery. I heard whining and glanced down: a black and tan puppy, leash tied to a post, tail in a frantic wag, greeting every person that passed by as it waited for its owner. And I thought about Suky, her simple, unconditional love for Adam. How much easier to be a dog than an idiotic, selfish, fucked-up human being.

My dad was getting out of his taxi as we arrived back at the house. He looked shattered but relieved to be home. I went over, and took his holdall. He nodded an acknowledgement at me, then at Adam. Claire abandoned the trunkful of beer to give Dad a hug.

"Was the trip back OK?" she asked.

"Fine," he said, and that was all. Later, no doubt, we'd hear all about the adventure of making it back across the choppy North Sea. The occasional news reports of helicopter fatalities made us ever aware of the very real dangers the riggers faced each time they took that trip, and we tried not to think about it. But once Dad had loosened up with a few beers, he'd turn it into a thrilling saga that sounded too far-fetched to be real, of ex-military pilots fighting to keep control of their craft in hundred-mile-an-hour headwinds, swells of up to twenty meters rolling below, the copter being thrown from side to side, pitching thirty feet in a second, rotor blades juddering. It was like reading a scene from a Wilbur Smith novel, and

I'd loved those stories when I was young, before I had any understanding of the fragility of life.

I took my father's bag inside, returning to help Adam bring in the crates of beer, not a word passing between us, even when I tripped over the bag, which I'd stupidly left right in our path. We deposited the beer next to my parents and their tight embrace, my mother sniffling against my father's shoulder. Yet more of my doing? Probably, but it wasn't mentioned. We dodged around them and followed Claire out to the garden—marginally more neutral territory than the living room. She'd thought ahead and collected three bottles of beer on her way through. She flicked off the caps and handed one to each of us.

"I'll drive," Adam offered. "I'll just have the one."

"Are you sure?" I asked.

"I'm sure."

I was grateful. Intoxicated was the only way I was going to make it through the day.

"So, this is Adam," my father said. He held out his hand. Adam shook it firmly.

"Good to meet you, Mr. Brooks."

"Dave," my father said. His name was, in fact, Alexander, but the riggers called him Dave and it stuck.

"Bet tells me you're a teacher."

"That's right," Adam confirmed.

"Sport?"

"Performing Arts."

"Right," my dad said, nodding, clearly no clue what that was, not that I'd be any the wiser if Adam hadn't explained it to me. Mostly he taught acting, with some directing thrown in, but he didn't look or behave like an actor. He was a physical, sporty, feet firmly on the ground kind of guy.

The rest of the day progressed in much the same way, conversations revolving around jobs and family, nothing so controversial as mine and Adam's relationship. To be fair to my dad, he was taking it—well—like a man, as in he was avoiding all the stuff he couldn't deal with, such as mine and Adam's relationship. I tried to follow his example, giving long, detailed answers to his questions about how my job with Magda was going. And drinking beer. Way too much beer.

We left late evening, though still early enough for Adam to grab a pint before last orders, and with an arrangement in place to meet up for dinner on Tuesday, which gave us a couple of days to go sightseeing, or whatever. I was too drunk to care, quite frankly. Back at the King's Head, Adam examined me doubtfully when I said I wanted a whisky. He ordered it anyway, along with a beer for himself, and got Jimmy to fill my glass to the top, with lemonade. I caught my scowling reflection in the mirror behind the bar as I took the glass from him, staggering a little. He grabbed my arm to steady me.

"Fresh air," he said. I shrugged, staggered again. We went out to the beer garden. My eyes weren't working properly, and I struggled to focus. So drunk. So what?

He was there again, sitting in the same corner as he had the previous night, watching as Adam talked close to my ear, and laughed at my protests that I was perfectly fine. I could barely get the words out and gave up trying after a while.

"Get 'em down you," Jimmy called. "Come on, folks." He circulated the tables, collecting empty glasses. It was almost eleven o'clock. He paused by our table. "Once this lot are gone I'll get you another, lads, all right?"

"Cheers, mate," Adam replied. I nodded, lolling on Adam's shoulder. I wanted to go to bed. My eyes sagged shut, and I listened to people making their way past us, back through the pub and out onto the road. Someone bumped into my arm as they passed. In fact they banged into me really hard. I turned, wobbling and almost sliding off the bench, trying to see who it was. He stared back at me, the hate coming off him in waves.

"What's the matter?"

It took a moment for me to register that Adam had asked the question. I turned around again, saw two of him.

"Hm?"

"Someone you know?"

"Uh. Yeah." I scrambled around in my brain, trying to make a sentence, but couldn't. "Key," I opted for, holding out my hand. Adam fished in his pocket and passed over our room key.

"I'll be up in sec," he said. I left, dragging myself up the stairs, clinging to the banister rail, the ascent to the second floor seemingly never-ending. Getting the key in the door was quite a trial, but I got there eventually, catapulted into the room, pulled off my sneakers and jeans and collapsed on the bed.

***

I awoke to the shrill song of blackbirds, and eye-stinging daylight, which, at this time of year could mean it was anywhere between four in the morning and ten at night. Adam was fast asleep in the bed beside me, his hands clasped under his cheek, his long, slow exhalations lifting my hair. I shivered, stretched a chilly arm out of the covers and felt around for my phone. Couldn't find it. I sat on the edge of the bed, instinctively putting my hand to my head in an attempt to mute the debilitating *thud-thud* against the inside of my skull, spotting my discarded jeans on the floor. Gingerly, I reached down and retrieved my phone from the pocket. 4:35 a.m. I felt like shit. Pulling myself to my feet was a further ordeal, but I needed to use the bathroom and brush my teeth to get rid of the horrendous taste in my mouth. I made it across the room, did the necessary and got back in one piece, wide awake now. I brought up the image of James on my phone, studying it, zooming in so I could seek out the little dimples he got in his cheeks when he smiled. I smiled back, remembering the conversation with my mother, and the realization that she'd walked in on us so many times that we hadn't known about. I'd sent James an email, telling him what she'd said. His reply?

Well, duh! She already knew.

Was he right? Had she known all along? I never got the chance to ask what made him think that, not that it mattered really. It wasn't my mother I'd been hiding from all these years. Of course I cared what she thought. I wanted her approval—all children, however horrific their upbringing, want their parents' love and acceptance; to make them proud. Not that I'm saying my parents were cruel—they were emotionally distant, but never cruel. No, I was hiding from the pain, the soul-crushing agony that kept catching me unawares, getting in the way of any chance Adam and I had of finding happiness. What he'd said about Bobby—about not laying down the law sooner—I could see now I was forcing him to make the same mistake again. Adam couldn't help me. No one could. I wanted Solemn Solomon back. I missed him, stoically flatlining through life, getting the job done. It was stupid to think I could be anything else, romanticizing that short period of freedom and happiness before James died, believing I could feel like that again. Adam deserved better, deserved to be happy. It was time for me to say goodbye, to both of them.

Chapter Twenty

Next time I awoke it was to the sound of voices, distant and mumbling, echoes deadened by carpets…I looked up at the familiar ceiling, the stark chrome spotlights. My feet were touching the wall at the end of the bed, feeling out the wallpaper join with my big toe. Claire was livid, understandably—not about the wallpaper. Who likes being woken up by their still slightly drunk (even now) and very miserable big brother at five in the morning? If I'd been she and she'd been me, I'd have slammed the door in my face, but thankfully she wasn't me, hence how I came to be here, in my old room. A knock came at the door. I groaned and pulled the pillow over my face. The door opened anyway.

"Hey."

Adam. My mother had let him upstairs, to my room. My, how the times they were a-changing. He tugged at the pillow. I kept my grip on it.

"I've been looking everywhere for you."

Yeah, well that couldn't have taken more than about ten minutes in a town like ours.

"I got Claire's number from Yvonne in the end."

So fucking what? That was the voice in my head, the teenage me. It must've been the environment—being back in my room, with my boyfriend. Flashback…

"Sol, please?"

"Please what?"

"Talk to me." He'd stopped fighting me for the pillow.

"There's nothing left to say."

He stopped fighting me for the words.

I was finding it difficult to breathe, but I didn't want to see his face as I said what I needed to. I'd lose my resolve. Even now, I could imagine those beautiful gray eyes staring into mine, confused, hurt. I didn't want to be the cause of that pain.

"I think we should go our separate ways," I said.

"You do." Not a question.

"Yeah, I do."

"Is it what you want?"

"What's that supposed to mean?"

"Exactly what I said. Do you want us to break up?"

No. I didn't, but what choice did I have? He snatched the pillow away and tossed it on the floor, his eyes locking with mine. I wanted to look away but I was trapped in his gaze, drowning in liquid silver.

"I shouldn't have left Elise."

A cruel thing to say? Indeed, I'd planned it that way—not to hurt him, but to make him walk away, run out of patience. Instead, he smiled.

"Sticks and stones." He leaned forward, kissing me gently. It sent a shiver all the way through me, in spite of everything. "You think you can break me that easily? I love you." He smoothed my forehead with light-touch fingertips. "Do you love me?"

I nodded, felt tears trickle down either side of my face. He wiped them away with his thumbs.

"Why did you insist we stay at the King's Head?"

"I didn't insist."

"No?"

"It was that, or stay here."

"There's a hotel a few miles out of town."

He was right. There was. Had I even considered that option? I honestly couldn't say, but at the very least I'd dismissed it on an unconscious level.

"The way I see it," he continued, "either you did it to sabotage our relationship, or you were trying to save it."

"Why would I want to sabotage it?"

"Perhaps because you think you're unworthy? Or I am? I don't know."

I felt so vulnerable, lying flat on my back, pinned down by my single quilt. I could move my arms to cover my face. I could turn my face away. Hell, I could've just closed my eyes. They were all physical possibilities, yet I knew that doing any of them meant so much more than the act itself. I would be breaking the connection between us.

"But then you tell me you love me," he said.

I blinked up at him. It meant "yes." Words would probably have made that clearer. However, they were a little beyond me right at that moment.

"Which means you want to try and save us."

I blinked again, forced my head to move in the affirmative. He sighed in frustration.

"I'm done with all the crap, Sol. I know it's only been four months, but we're either doing this, or we're not."

Ah, *there's* my Captain Impatient. I sensed an ultimatum coming.

"Straight-talking time. Do you want to break up?"

"No."

"Do you love me?"

"Yes."

"Do you want to fix this?"

"Yes."

"OK." He put a hand on either side of me, so that now I really was pinned down, and he kissed me slowly but deeply. My resistance gave up resisting. I kissed back. He moved away from the bed and pulled the covers off. I was wearing only boxer shorts, my erection already tenting the jersey fabric. He smirked. "We can deal with that later. You need to visit the cemetery."

"What for? I have no trouble accepting he's dead. Seeing his grave isn't going to change anything."

"Your guilt. I don't know why you blame yourself for James's death, because you keep avoiding it, refuse to talk about it. I do understand that's how you feel, but it's screwing with us."

"Adam, I—"

"You need to visit the cemetery," he repeated, passing me my clothes, and then standing back, watching me expectantly. I sighed and pulled myself into a sitting position. At least my head wasn't banging anymore. He waited long enough to see me shove my legs into my jeans.

"I'll be downstairs," he said. "Don't run away. Again."

Not funny. He left. I finished dressing and went to use the bathroom. I bumped into my father on the way back.

"Morning," he said.

"Hi, Dad. Sleep well?"

"Other than some idiot hammering on the door in the middle of the night."

"Ah. Sorry." I looked down at my feet. Thirty-one years old—you'd think I'd have the whole acting-like-an-adult thing nailed. A hand landed heavy on my shoulder.

"It's nothing to be ashamed of," my father said.

I lifted my head and frowned, unsure if he meant what I thought he did. Too much to hope for?

"Being homosexual," he added.

Huh.

"There's a couple of lads on the rig, get ribbed mercilessly, they do. And being the boss, I have to intervene. It used to make me uncomfortable saying something, because it's all banter, you know? 'Backs to the wall, fellas, Smithy's coming through.' Just banter. And then your mate, James…"

"Boyfriend," I corrected, my chest tightening at what had been an instinctive admission, because I'd never had "that conversation" with my dad, not about the birds and the bees, or about being gay. Nothing. Three months on the rigs, a month at home—he was around a lot more than most people's dads, I supposed, but we didn't have that sort of relationship. It made what he was doing now all the more meaningful.

"Aye," he said. "Boyfriend." He turned away from me and headed off for the bathroom, newspaper tucked under his arm. One hand on the door, he stopped and looked back. "Sorry, son. You've had a rough do of it." He went inside, slid the bolt.

I remained where I was, dazed, until Adam called up, "You coming?"

I shook myself out of it and went downstairs, right into his waiting arms, aware of my mother watching from the kitchen. He smiled and hugged me tight.

"You're not going to run away this time?"

"I'll try not to," I said.

***

The cemetery was how I'd expected—quiet, with one or two people delivering bunches of flowers to graves of loved ones. I'd always thought it was a bit pointless. I mean, what do the dead care for flowers? Still, I felt naked in my empty-handedness, and cold, in spite of the sun that was strong enough to turn my bare arms pink. Adam walked at my side, though not too close, and it was I who sought out his hand, lacing my fingers through his. He glanced my way, wordlessly. I kept my focus on him, aware that James's grave was just up ahead of us. I wasn't sure I could bear to see it, but as we got closer the profusion of color drew my attention. I faltered. Adam kept moving forward, gently pulling me along, until I was standing on the path in front of the plot. I gazed down in awe. Every single inch of it was covered with vibrant, fresh flowers, so many colors, so beautiful. I was speechless.

"Yvonne said people come visiting all the time," Adam explained. "It's always like this."

I thought about it, and it made complete sense to me. James was a popular guy—friendly, loving, open, but also flamboyant and outrageous in every way—his clothes, the things he said, the way he said them. Just like Calvin with his LGBT buttons, James sent out the message, loud and clear. No two ways about it, he was gay. You could love him, or hate him. Most, it would seem, chose to love him, because unlike Cal, James was warm, kind, compassionate. He didn't deserve to die. He had so much to give.

"You've not been here before, have you?" Adam asked. I shook my head. "So you haven't seen the inscription on the headstone?"

I glanced at it briefly, taking in that it was black granite, a rainbow inlaid into the arched top, James's name beneath it, along with his photo. It was one I'd never seen before, and I stepped around the flowers to get a better view. He was smiling, always smiling, the little dimples in his cheeks just visible. His expression was cheeky, flirtatious, his eyes looking up and to the right, rather than at the camera. I followed their direction, past the headstone, up into clear blue sky. Nothing there. I don't know what I was expecting, but I was still disappointed. I returned my gaze to the headstone. And that was when I saw it, lurking just behind the rainbow.

"You know that Sol means 'sun' in Spanish, don't you?"

"So you keep saying."

"Which means you're not allowed to be a grump. You'll turn my blue skies cloudy."

"Let's go blow those clouds away," I whispered.

I'd left Adam at the end of the grave, but now he moved closer and put his arms around me from behind. I grabbed them, held on tight.

"After you moved to the States," he said, "Claire told James's parents about you, and they weren't surprised. He thought the world of you. When they had the headstone made, they wanted to acknowledge that you'd lost someone special too."

I started to cry.

"The song is for you, Sol."

"The song?"

I hadn't got as far as reading the rest of the inscription, which was in smaller, cursive letters, rendered blurry and illegible by my tears. I wiped my eyes and moved closer. Adam kept hold of me, thank God, because if he hadn't I'd have collapsed and crushed the flowers.

> *Don't you cry, you will see bye and bye,*
> *that a rainbow bright will shine on high,*
> *there are always rain clouds in the sky,*
> *and I'll tell you sweetheart why:*
> *'Cause it takes a little rain with the sunshine,*
> *like the tear drops come with the smiles;*
> *but the troubles never come all at one time,*
> *just wait a little while, remember,*
> *flowers couldn't grow without rain, dear,*
> *happiness we share with the pain, dear,*
> *'cause it takes a little rain with the sunshine*
> *to make the world go around.*

Chapter Twenty-One

On the drive back to the King's Head my mind kept going over and over the first two lines of that song: "Don't you cry, you will see bye and bye, that a rainbow bright will shine on high…" I'd taken a photo of the headstone, in case I should ever forget, but that whole rainbow thing? The freedom flag, they called it, right? James and I were on our own, two boys trying to love, in a town that, to me, had always been infused with hate.

I chucked the T-shirt back at Calvin.
"It's gaudy and stupid. I'm not wearing it."
"Your opinion is not important. The colors are symbolic. The pink—"
"Pink schmink. Mix them all together, and what do you get? White-out, that's what."

See, love wasn't a freedom to me. It was a prison I'd refused to enter. Yet all those flowers on James's grave, the messages of love and acceptance that accompanied them—I could see now that I had allowed a miniscule, ignorant minority to control my life. My mum, bless her, with her obsession with AIDS, my dad, and George, being pushed to the frontline of a battle no one should have to fight, and Elise, whom I had perceived to be the enemy, when we were cabinmates, cowering in a dark corner, hiding from ourselves. That was real homophobia: fear of losing a child, a friend, a parent, a lover. What those animals did to James wasn't an act of fear. It was an act of violence, of hatred. Calvin would've ripped off their balls, put them on display for all to see. James would've forgiven them. Me? On this occasion I was inclined to side with Cal.

I was standing at the bar, not entirely sure how I'd got there. Adam stood next to me, talking to Jimmy, their conversation an indecipherable nonsense as I watched Yvonne watching me. I could feel her sadness, her love.

"Can I talk to you, please?" I asked, a sob escaping with the words. I walked off, toward the stairs, leaning against the wall, trying to regain some control, aware of Yvonne standing next to me, gently rubbing my back and shushing me. So much for talking. I could hardly catch my breath.

"Come up to the flat," she suggested, leading me by the hand up the stairs and through the door marked "Private," into the Coolican home. She sat me on the sofa, disappeared, returned with a box of tissues. "I'll make us a cup of tea," she said and left me again. I sniffed and sobbed, trying to find distractions in the room around me, but everywhere I looked James stared back. School photos, professional portraits, a large print of the picture on his headstone, an artist's impression. I couldn't escape his watchful gaze, those blue sky eyes like blazing sapphires, cold and hard, judgmental of my lies, my denial of how much he meant to me. I had loved him, and abandoned him, then abandoned myself.

Yvonne returned with the tea, handed me a cup and sat next to me.

"You've been to visit James?" she asked. I nodded. The tears started again. "Adam said he was going to take you. He went looking for you this morning, and when he came back he asked me about the song."

"Claire told you?"

"Yes, she did. She told us everything. James adored you. He never stopped talking about you. We always thought it was one-sided, until Claire explained the way your mum reacted."

"I adored him too," I said. Kind of said. I was crying too hard to speak properly, but Yvonne somehow got the gist.

"I know you did, sweetheart. When you arrived here with Adam on Saturday, I was surprised only because I knew you'd married a woman, and you went to such lengths to convince people you were straight whenever you came home. I thought maybe Claire got it wrong."

I laughed through my tears, not out of joy, or because I thought it was funny. I think it was just out of relief at finally being able to let go of my grief.

"Adam is wonderful," I said. "He's the best thing that ever happened to me."

"That's exactly what he said about you."

"Did he?"

She nodded. "He sat right where you're sitting now, telling me how he fell in love with you the minute he set eyes on you."

"He said that?" I was sure she was making it up to try and jolly me along.

"We were laughing at how it sounded like a story in a magazine—love at the checkout."

OK, so maybe she wasn't making it up then.

"Did he tell you he tried to push in?"

She chuckled. "No. He left out that part."

I shook my head, and smiled. I was starting to feel a little better, a little more like me. Confession time.

"I finished things with James after I thought my mum had caught us together. She's always been so opinionated, and there was all the stuff in the news about AIDS when we were growing up. I think she honestly thought that you got it just by being gay."

"Oh, I know. We've heard it all before, Sol. Some of the things people said when James came out, because, as you know, he did it in style. They soon changed their tune after he was killed."

"They need shooting, the fucking lot of them." My anger flared so suddenly and violently that it frightened me. With a bit of a struggle, I pushed it back down inside. "Sorry," I said.

"It's all right. It's perfectly normal to be angry, but you also need to know when to let go. We were angry for a long, long time. We used to think that if they caught the boys who did it we'd finally get peace of mind, leave the anger and hatred behind, but it fades, and James's death wasn't all in vain. It made people think, question their beliefs. A lot of the regulars in here, for instance, used to be so hateful, but not anymore."

"It shouldn't take someone dying to change people's minds."

"True enough." Yvonne sipped her tea, waiting for me to say more, and there was so much more I wanted to say. Whether it was wise to do so was an entirely different matter.

"I was scared," I admitted.

"That's understandable."

"No, I don't mean of being beaten up, or at least I was scared I'd get beaten up, which is why I started kickboxing and working out. I was scared that people would judge me, hate me, just because of what I am. James was a much stronger person than me."

"I hope you know better now than to care what people like that think."

"Yeah, I do, but it took meeting Adam for me to realize."

"You got there in the end, that's all that matters."

I nodded, glancing around the room again. Those eyes weren't judging me quite so harshly now. One more confession to make, and I was done. My plan was to gradually build up to it, lay some groundwork, not just so it didn't come as a shock to Yvonne. I despised myself for concealing it all these years and wasn't sure I could cope with allowing it to the surface, but like she'd said, there's a time to let go.

"I know who killed James," I blurted. Absolutely nothing like a gradual build-up. Way to go.

"We all have our suspicions, Sol."

"But if you were able to prove who it was?"

She shook her head. "Nothing's going to bring him back."

I clamped my teeth together. I'd told her as much as I needed to. I'd just wanted to see her response, to try and decide how to act on what I knew. I drank the rest of my tea.

"I'd best get back to Adam," I said. We hugged. "Thank you for listening to me, and for the inscription. I'm truly honored, not that I deserve to be that important."

"What nonsense!"

She was quite cross with me, but it was the truth. I'd betrayed James in the worst way imaginable.

Bruised and battle-weary, I retired to our room and sat on the end of the bed, looking out across the green hills, absently tallying sheep. The door opened behind me, strong, warm arms encircled me, holding me tight, holding me together.

"Thank you," I said. Adam kissed the top of my head.

"I'm going to buy a pair of handcuffs for you."

I turned to look at his face up close. He was smirking. I smiled.

"Kinky!"

"Isn't it?" He kissed me again. "You OK?"

I thought for a moment, nodded. "I'm OK."

***

We spent the rest of the afternoon lying on the bed together, making tentative plans for the move back to England. In the occasional pauses in our dialogue, I considered the enormity of what we were doing. Boston had been my home for eight years, and I'd worked at Magda for almost as long. That, really, was the only part I was going to miss. I loved my job, I loved working with George, but she wouldn't be around forever. In fact, it occurred to me that she'd pushed for the second design team to train me up for her job. I was sure she'd understand I hadn't meant to let her down.

The chatter of the first wave of evening customers floated up to us, and we decided to go out for a walk, stopping by the fish and chip shop, I'm not sure why—we were both already suffering for the lapse in our diet and exercise regimen.

"I'm getting flabby," Adam said, dumping the last of his supper in the trash and patting his very firm and unflabby abs.

"Yeah, right!"

"I am! Feel." He lifted his T-shirt and pressed my hand to his belly, flexing against my fingers.

"I guess you could do with a little toning up," I said.

"Uh huh? We should definitely work out tonight."

"Definitely," I agreed, kissing him. An older man and woman getting into their car across the street didn't give us a second glance. I could've taken it as evidence for what Yvonne had said—that James's death had made a difference—but that's not what I saw. In this town, this *small* town, where everyone was aware of everyone else's business, people would have known who James's attackers were. Family members would surely have questioned whereabouts when asked for alibis on the night that James Coolican was fatally wounded, would have wondered about blood-stained clothes. Why didn't anyone say anything? Do anything? Do *something*?

"Sol, wait!"

I was running, I discovered at the sound of Adam's voice far behind me. I was running away. From me.

Chapter Twenty-Two

"Get off me!" I tried to break free of Adam's iron grip on my arms. How the fuck he'd got me to the ground I'll never know, but that's where I was, with his hands crushing my wrists. He was sitting on my chest, and I used my lower body to try and roll him off. He was one strong bastard.

"What the hell are you doing?" he asked. He looked angry and bewildered.

"Let me go."

"Oh no. No way. We're going to have this out, right here, right now."

"Adam! Please?"

"No, Sol. I'm done chasing you. If I let you go and you run away again, that's it. Done."

He eased off on my wrists a little. I knew better than to fight back.

I said, "I know who killed James."

"You think you know…"

"I *know* who killed James. I've got evidence."

"You've…" He released my wrists completely. He was still sitting on me, though, and now he'd leaned back I was finding it difficult to breathe. "What evidence?"

"Text messages."

"Explain."

"Can I get up, please?"

"No!"

"If you let me up, I'll show you."

I watched him consider my proposition. He slowly lifted a leg clear, grabbing one of my wrists again as he did so.

"I'm getting those fucking handcuffs," he muttered, not entirely joking. I swear I had never been like this in my life. I didn't know what was wrong with me, but I was beginning to think I might need to see a shrink. I dug my phone out of my pocket, opting for the original messages, copied from phone to phone over the past eleven years. I also had back-ups, and back-ups of back-ups, the printed version in a box of letters in Elise's apartment. I opened the first message I'd received and passed my phone to Adam.

"There's about thirty of them, just scroll down," I said. If I sounded matter-of-fact, it was because I knew this was the end of the line. He was already scrolling, and scrolling, and scrolling. His eyes widened, his mouth dropped open, the color left his face.

"Oh my God," he gasped. He was still scrolling, blinking, head shaking, disbelief, outrage, fury, then, "Oh my God," again.

And as I stood there, watching him reading those text messages, I felt violated, like a part of me was being slashed and beaten, just as James had been. My own fault. I'd kept them to myself when I should've gone straight to the police. Their names were attached to the messages, but it was unlikely they'd still have those numbers now. I'd withheld evidence. How fucking stupid and selfish of me. Not only had I blown any chances of proving that it was them, I'd lost Adam too. I could see it, in his horrified expression.

He reached the end of the messages, slowly turning to face me.

"I wish…" I began, I think, to say, that I wished it had been me who had died, or I wished I could take it back, or…I don't know. The fierceness of Adam's embrace knocked the thought right out of me. He was sobbing, and apologizing, and we were standing in the middle of the high road of my home town on a Monday evening, and it was all so surreal. Why was he telling me he was sorry? I contemplated giving him a slap, you know the way they do in old movies when women come over all hysterical? I decided against it, thought he'd probably knock me out with one punch.

It took a lot of effort for Adam to stop crying. It seemed I'd been crying too, but I really wasn't connected to my body, like I was inside a spacesuit, or something, and now Adam was telling me he loved me, and wiping my cheeks with his thumbs, staring deep into my eyes. Lights on, no one home.

We were back in our room, washing faces, getting jackets. We were sitting in a car, my sister was driving. We were in the living room of my parents' house, and there were police. I was talking, they were writing, Adam was holding my hand. Claire was holding my hand. Mum was crying. Dad brought cups of tea.

"I wish Suky was here," I said.

***

I rolled over to check the time on my phone, wondering why my alarm hadn't gone off. No phone. So tired, must have stayed up late drinking. What was I doing last night? It ripped through me like a rush of icy wind, and I gasped, sat up suddenly.

"Adam!"

"Hey," he answered me sleepily. "I'm here. It's OK."

Oh, thank God. I lay down again, moving closer so I could wrap myself in his warmth. A bad dream?

"You should still be out for the count," he said.

"Huh?"

"The pills the doctor gave you. He said they'd knock you out."

"Pills?" That would explain why I felt like I'd been hit by a truck.

"You need anything?"

That was the last thing I remembered.

***

"Good morning."

He kissed me on the forehead. Very paternal. I frowned.

"Yvonne's going to bring our breakfasts up."

"Um…" In my head the phrase went, "What the fuck is going on?" My mouth didn't want to play along.

Time passed. There was a knock at the door. Adam got up and answered it.

"How is he?"

Me?

"OK. A bit groggy."

"Understandable. How are you holding up?"

"Fine, thanks. You?"

"Same. I'll let you go."

The door closed.

"Sit up, handsome."

That was me too. I shuffled up the bed, with much effort. My eyelids needed props.

"What were they?" I asked.

"What were what?"

"Pills."

"Oh. Valium."

"Why?"

"You were…very agitated."

Hm. So agitated I couldn't remember anything about it. I ate slowly, feeling very heavy. The room tilted a little. I grabbed hold of Adam's arm. He dropped his fork.

"You OK?" he asked. He looked worried.

"Yeah. Dizzy."

***

As the morning wore on, the effect of the drugs wore off, and I remembered what had happened the day before: visiting James's grave, the song, talking to Yvonne, showing Adam the text messages. I knew I'd spoken to the police, but couldn't recall what was said. Claire phoned to check we were in—we were sitting in the smaller of the two rooms of the pub. She came to visit.

"They got three of them," she said.

"Who?" I asked.

She frowned. "The police."

I rubbed my eyes. "What?"

"The police got three of the men who attacked James and threatened you."

Oh, *them*! Of course! Claire hugged me and started crying. All these tears. It was like being at a funeral.

After Claire had gone, I shrugged at Adam. "I don't know what the fuck is happening," I said. "Why haven't I been arrested?"

"Why would you be arrested?"

"What's it called? Perverting the course of justice."

"You're the victim."

"No, James was…"

"Sol." Adam's lips pressed to mine, stopping me from protesting further. Not helpful. My brain was misfiring all over the place. He moved away.

"Victim?"

"Death threats."

I nodded slowly. It had never occurred to me before, but I suppose that's what they were.

> *You saw what we did to your faggy friend. Your turn next.*
>
> *Gonna fuck you queers before you can fuck us.*

"Do those pills cause hallucinations?" I asked.

"No idea," Adam said. "Why?"

"Because I'm sure my parents just walked in."

He looked toward the door and waved. My parents came over. Mum hugged Adam.

Mum hugged Adam.

Wow. My mum just hugged my boyfriend. I got up, staggered a little. He caught me.

"Hi, Mum," I said, sounding pathetic and small—not an act. She hugged me and my dad gave me a swift embrace, followed up by a good, solid pat on the back. Madness!

"Feeling better, son?" my dad asked.

"Yeah, thanks." I had no idea if it were true. My dad went to the bar, returning with pints of bitter for Adam and himself, a glass of wine for my mum and I got to have a Coke. Awesome.

We chatted. No. *They* chatted. I sat nodding like a bobble-headed bull dog toy on a parcel shelf.

"We've postponed dinner, darling," Mum said.

"Dinner?" I queried.

"With Claire and John. The booking is for tomorrow now, at six, as they're driving home afterwards, but if you're not up to it—"

"I'll be fine, Mum."

Yeah, so…talk about entering the twilight zone.

Adam and Dad went to get another drink. Mum reached across and squeezed my hand. She didn't say the word, she kind of transmitted it telepathically. She was sorry, I wasn't sure what for, but figured it was probably something to do with, well, everything. I squeezed back.

"Have you got your dress for the wedding?" I asked.

She sighed loudly. "No. Honestly, Solly, you have no idea of the trouble I'm having finding something."

And she was off. I listened, smiling to myself, because she sounded just like me, so maybe it was nothing to do with being an engineer after all. Don't get me wrong, our relationship was far from fixed, but it was…better. Much better than it had been in a long time. In fact, since the fateful "Gay like Freddie Mercury" conversation. As for Adam and my dad, or Adam and my mum, or Adam and Claire, Yvonne, Jimmy, the world…I'd yet to meet anyone who didn't get on with Adam, and griped as much in jest when we were in bed and finally, finally alone.

Chapter Twenty-Three

On Wednesday morning, still fuzzy from the tranqs, I forced myself out of bed to go for a run with Adam, mostly because I was feeling uncharacteristically clingy. However, that soon dissipated once we were out in the open. The early morning air was wonderfully cool and refreshing. We jogged through low cloud, the microscopic droplets of moisture accumulating on our faces, dripping from our chins, and down our necks. I was finding it quite a trial to keep up, so we alternated between running, jogging and walking, pausing to watch a collie dog steer a herd of sheep into the distant misty hills, before we jogged back to the King's Head. Yvonne was already toiling away in the kitchen—another couple had arrived the previous evening and we greeted each other with a friendly "good morning," settling at a table in the beer garden with our glasses of orange juice. Not that we were being antisocial—the beer garden was a sun trap, where we could make the most of the beautiful morning, and a minute or so later the other couple followed our lead.

The food and exercise invigorated me, helped along in no small part by having faced up to the baggage that had been dragging me down for so long it was a wonder I didn't walk with a stoop. Needless to say, I was up for a spot of very personal attention and was *almost* reaching Adam's level of well-practiced impatience, waiting out my turn for the shower. By the time I was done, he was dressed.

"Ha! I don't think so," I said. I grabbed him by the waistband of the jeans he'd just put on, unzipped them and freed him from his boxers. He spread his feet apart, granting me access to his balls. I opened my lips wider, trying to fit them in my mouth too, tickling him awake with my tongue, easing back as he sprang to life. His hand was on my head, resting gently, no pushing, allowing me to control the speed and the depth, which was a little frustrating. I was in the mood for some hard, hot action, but my captain was taking it nice and steady this morning. I lifted the hem of his T-shirt, an unspoken request that he remove it. He did so. I ran my hands up over his abs, reaching his nipples with the tips of my fingers. He started to grind his hips. I brought my hands back down and grabbed his ass, pulling him deeper down my throat, breathing through my nose, the air ruffling his pubes, making it seem as if that little tattooed cat was prancing right in front of my face. Adam watched, that crooked smile telling me he was enjoying it as much as I was. I could honestly have carried on forever, with his taste and his scent filling my mouth and nose. I eased back, sucking hard, plunged again. He pulled away and shook his head.

"Too close," he said. I got to my feet, his hand immediately wrapping around my dick, his warm fist delivering a tantalizingly slow squeezing tug. "Get on the bed," he instructed. Aye, sir. He kicked his legs out of his half-mast jeans and sidled up alongside. I reached out for him. He captured my arm, commencing a trail of kisses that started at my fingers, detoured to explore my mouth, continuing down to my nipples, pausing to circle them with his tongue, sucking each in turn, until they stood, proud buoys marking the rocks in my ocean. He climbed aboard, navigating that familiar yet treacherous route, as I, the long-lost Marie Celeste, finally made port in the rolling calm before the glorious storm.

With each upward thrust his abs tensed, highlighting the outlines of the individual muscles. A week of carbs, beer and no workouts had given him a little bit of a belly, I supposed, though not much, and as he moved I noticed the faintest of crinkles in his skin. I ran my fingers over them, fascinated. Early thirties wasn't that old, but we weren't getting any younger—obviously. I smiled at how silly that was, and how wonderful it would be, years from now, still doing this. Would we look like our dads? Warren was a big man, and I could see Adam now, with a sprinkling of gray at his temples framing those sultry silver eyes, my sexy-hot cuddly man, keeping me warm through the English winter nights. As for me? I couldn't visualize what I'd look like, but Adam had already seen me at my worst, and he was still here, making love to me. His dick beckoned my attention, swooping low before him, bobbing with the motion. He pushed down again, forcing me deep inside him, his smile lingering awhile, eyes half-shut. He craned to kiss me, the change in angle intensifying the squeeze around me. I groaned with pleasure. I was trying to hold out, but I was on the edge. I reached for him. He shook his head.

"Let go," he said. He increased his speed, knowing I was at the point where resistance was impossible. I lifted to meet his down with my up, a relentless tide surging through me, heading for shore, now crashing into the rocks with explosive force. I swam for the surface, gulping for air. I was done.

Adam lifted himself clear, shifting as if to move to my side. I grabbed him, steered him by his dick so that he had to shuffle up the bed, his knees either side of me, coming to a stop under my arms. I lifted my head to collect the clear nectar oozing from his slit. He shifted again, repositioning himself so that he could hold the headboard and fuck my mouth. It lasted no more than thirty seconds, spurts of come landing in my mouth, on my lips, my cheeks, *in my hair*! A couple more thrusts and he moved away, returning with tissue to wipe me clean, or what was left to wipe away. I was still horny, and I'd licked what I could reach. He flushed the tissues, returned one last time and flopped down next to me. I rolled into the crook of his arm, and we kissed, gentle pecks interspersed with deeper kisses.

"We should go and do some sightseeing," he suggested once normality returned. I shrugged indifferently. The sights here were plenty good enough for me, but I went along with his wishes. I washed my hair (not making that mistake twice) and we shaved and dressed so that we could go straight from our day trip to dinner, heading out for a two-hundred-year-old working waterwheel at a long-derelict grinding mill, where I bored Adam into a coma with my commentary on how these things worked. He took it like a man. He may even have called me "dear."

After that, we went to "Ye Olde Tea Room," which didn't look especially "olde," was a warehouse rather than a room, and sold more coffee than the average Starbucks. Adam and I did have tea, though—cream tea, with scones stuffed with whipped cream and strawberries—not the best substitute for our much-missed vanilla cream protein shakes, and delicious for about one bite. I pushed my plate away. Adam's eyes narrowed disapprovingly.

"Are you going to eat tonight?" he asked.

"Hey! I don't see you making any progress either." If I was being defensive, it was because I knew he was right. I'd lost weight since we'd been in England, from being stressed, and not eating, and not being able to work out. Where Adam needed to train to stay slim, I'd always done it to bulk up. Without weight training, I'd have reverted to my former scrawny self. Again, my mind cast forward to our future, two contented old men, gone completely to seed because there was no need to impress anymore, toddling around a farmyard, tending chooks, cocoa at bedtime, big, hairy old man ears...I started chuckling to myself. Adam raised an eyebrow.

"What's funny?"

"Nothing. I was just picturing us in our twilight years."

"Twilight years?"

"You know, growing old together?"

"Together," Adam repeated.

I peered up at the bare steel rafters. "I think there's an echo in here." I returned my gaze to Adam. Those mercury orbs burned right into my mind, my soul.

"Yeah," he said. "I heard it too." He sounded like he'd been running.

"Are you all right?" I asked. He nodded and lifted my hand to his lips, his eyes still locked with mine. I could feel his pulse under my fingertips. It was racing.

"Never better," he said, giving me the most amazing smile. I melted to goo. "You?"

"Never better," I replied breathlessly.

Oh, I don't know. Maybe it was the after-effects of the tranquilizers.

***

Our dinner date venue was an all-you-can-eat carvery, with a self-service heated counter running half the perimeter of the very large dining room, and a friendly, casual atmosphere. Claire and John had already arrived and were seated in the back left corner. We headed over.

"John, you remember my brother, Sol," Claire introduced. We'd met once, back in the early days of their relationship, so I didn't really know the guy. We shook hands. "And this is Sol's partner, Adam," my sister finished.

"Good to meet you," Adam said graciously, also shaking John's hand, then exchanging an affectionate cheek kiss and embrace with Claire.

"Everything OK?" she asked far too brightly and not directed at me. She and John returned to their seats. Adam and I sat opposite each other, me next to John, Adam next to Claire. I smiled sweetly at her.

"I'm fine, thank you for asking."

Adam stamped on my foot and tried to pass it off as an accident. I wasn't going to cause a scene, but I didn't want them all worrying about me freaking out again. I really was fine, or getting there, anyway.

A waiter came over, took our drinks orders and explained how the food worked—get a plate, pile it on, eat, repeat until you have a coronary. He came back a few minutes later with our parents and our drinks; Dad sat on my right, Mum on Adam's left. He pulled the same cheek kiss greeting on her. She seemed delighted. OK, maybe I would need to take a raincheck on the *not* freaking out. This was beyond weird. How had we gone from only just being civil, to peace, love and harmony in thirty-six hours?

As per the waiter's instructions, we went and filled our plates at the counter. However, the minute I sat down to eat— surprise, surprise—I wasn't even the remotest bit hungry. Still, I made an effort, and listened to the conversations taking place around me. Mum and Claire were talking weddings across Adam, who was in turn telling John about his job. My dad said something. I didn't quite catch it.

"Hm?"

"When are you flying back to Boston?"

"Oh. Erm, Saturday morning." If he was trying to make small talk, something was amiss, and it was probably me. I attempted to reciprocate. "When are you back on the rig?"

"Three weeks Friday."

End of conversation, for us. The others continued for a while, but things were getting a little heated in some quarters. The wedding planning conversation slowly petered out, leaving just one person talking, more's the pity.

"That's not *really* being a teacher, is it?" John said, his tone pompous and more than a little pugnacious. Adam shrugged neutrally.

"No, I suppose it's more lecturing than teaching."

"Of course, there's not much call for actors in the *real* world."

I glanced across at Claire, noticed the pleading look in her eyes. Great. It was down to me to do the bailing out this time.

Alas, there was a hole in my bucket and the words dropped out the bottom before I had time to think them through.

"Guess what?" I said. "We're moving back to England."

My mother paused mid-chew, staring me down. She gently and deliberately set her fork on her plate, resumed masticating, and slowly turned to Adam. Had she reached the point of swallowing before John said what he did, I'm pretty sure she'd have come down on the pair of us like a ton of hyper-critical bricks.

"England?" he repeated, as if he'd never heard of such a place. He scoffed. "Well, they've cut *all* the performing arts budgets *here*."

That overstressing certain words thing he did was irritating.

"There's no jobs. It's a shame you're not a *proper* teacher. There's always plenty of supply work."

Really irritating.

On the plus side, it looked like my mother was now siding with Adam. My dad, Claire and I kept our heads down, shoveling food into our mouths as if this were the last meal we'd ever eat. Judging by Adam's and my mother's expressions it could well be. My mother was furious, and Adam? He didn't get angry often. Annoyed? Yes. Frustrated? Definitely. Impatient? And then some! But I could see him struggling to keep his breathing under control, his nostrils flaring wide with the effort. His leg jiggled against mine under the table. I reached under and squeezed his knee. He gave me a quick smile.

"You coming for more food, John?" my sister asked.

"Oh, no thanks, *sweet*. I'm fine for now."

Yeah, for now. John's gaze returned to Adam. I had no option but to engage him.

"What is it you teach again, John?"

"Mathematics."

"High school?"

"Yes, that's *right*, Sol."

Well done, clever boy. Have a gold star.

"That must be very rewarding," I said.

"Yes, it is."

Huh. I could have got him to count how many fucks I gave. All none of them. But I persevered, for the sake of peace.

"Do you need a math degree to teach it?" I asked.

"Not necessarily *maths*, but a *relevant* degree. I would think, if you were interested, your degree would *probably* be enough, with a teaching qualification, *obviously*."

Like I'd ever consider teaching high school kids. I'd rather go back to Elise. I wondered what she was doing now, started calculating the time difference…

"…I can email you the link," John finished.

"Yeah, thanks. I'll take a look," I said. "I think I'll, err, get some dessert." I made a quick getaway. Half a minute later my dad joined me.

"He's a bloody arsy bugger tonight," he remarked. We both watched our family from a distance. John had resumed his unprovoked, though by now rather benign attack on Adam.

"He's not normally like that?"

My dad shook his head and chuckled. "Your poor mum."

I switched my attention from Adam to my mother. She was still seething.

"I think she's a bit disappointed," my dad observed. Disappointed, seething—I suppose that's kind of the same thing. Or not. Lucky my dad worked away as much as he did, really, or we'd be searching under the patio for his remains.

"Why?" I asked, expecting him to say something about how I'd let her down big time, what, with my failed marriage and giving up my career to return to the UK.

"It would've been nice to see her future sons-in-law getting along."

OK. Very much not within expected parameters. Did she really see Adam that way?

"Of course," my dad continued, completely oblivious to the effect his words had had on me, "John's having work troubles of his own. Nothing personal. Your Adam's a decent lad, gets on with everyone…"

Drifting, slowly drifting. There goes my reality.

"Sol?"

"Hm?"

"Fudge cake?"

"Oh. Yeah. Please." I tuned in again, accepted the large slab of chocolate cake, trying very hard to ignore the crazy. We returned to the table.

"The *other* option…"

Oh God, was he still harping on? That nasal twang was seriously starting to grate on my nerves.

"…is to retrain in something *useful*, like…"

OK. Enough already.

"By the way," I said, swiveling to face my future-if-he-survives-tonight brother-in-law, "did Adam tell you he turned down a job at *Harvard*?"

Bam! Gotcha!

And the chocolate fudge cake turned out to be rather good after all.

Chapter Twenty-Four

All the way back to the King's Head, Adam kept doing that head-shaking, eyes to the sky thing that's supposed to signify disapproval, but failed because he was grinning like the Cheshire cat. To give John his due, he did apologize for being obnoxious and ruining our evening. I didn't think it had been that bad. It was actually quite a useful distraction from the fact that, mixed with my previously repressed grief, I was now starting to get cold feet about leaving Boston. I didn't mention any of this to Adam. He was already being overprotective when I really wasn't that fragile.

It was quiz night in the pub and busy, but Yvonne still spotted us through the crowd and held up an empty glass by way of asking if we wanted a drink. I confirmed we did as we passed on our way upstairs to exchange our shirts for T-shirts.

Or that was our intention.

Adam turned the key and frowned. "We mustn't have locked it."

The door opened on a dark room, which was odd, as it was still light outside, and we hadn't closed the curtains. He walked across to the window and pulled them open. I stepped in, stopped dead. Adam turned back, saw what I saw.

I knew for certain that we'd made the bed before we left, but it wasn't made now. The duvet was pulled right back, the sheet creased as if someone had been lying on it. And there, in the middle of the mattress, was a big, stinking pile of shit, with a knife jammed through it.

I moved closer, holding my nose and squinting to see what was underneath it.

"Sol, don't…"

Too late.

It was a copy of the photo from James's headstone.

I crossed the room, shoved Adam to one side, yanked the window open, looked down, saw *him* sitting there, looking right back at me. Fucking smiling. I flew from the room and down the stairs, tripped, kept going, straight through the pub out into the beer garden, grabbed him round the throat with one hand and lifted him out of his chair by his neck. His pint glass fell, smashing on the concrete slabs.

"You filthy, murderous, piece of shit!"

He spat in my face. I squeezed harder, moved in, my nose squashed against his.

"I'll fucking rip you apart for what you did."

"You're bloody mental," he said, laughing like he didn't know what I was talking about. He looked past me, I don't know what for. Likely allies, maybe. That just made me madder. He stamped on my foot, grabbed my arm with both hands, trying to pull me off. I was going to kill him. Strangle the bastard, make him suffer the way he'd made us suffer. He was choking, turning blue. His nails dug into my wrist, and I let go, punched him in the face, in the stomach. He raised his arms to protect himself. I knocked them away. He came at me. I backed off, kicked him in the balls, brought my knee up into his face, saw blood and spit arc through the air, got hold of his hair and slammed his head into the table, lifted it to do it again. The scum-sucking bastard was still calling me. Why wouldn't he just shut the fuck up? He had his hands inside his jacket, scrabbling around. I slammed him against the table again, yanked his head up and right back, saw a glint of reflected light. Another fucking knife. I couldn't move my arm.

"Sol! Stop!"

The knife lunged. I tried to grab the hand holding it to stop it, but I wasn't quick enough. I heard a yelp, turned, saw Adam stagger backwards.

"No!"

I picked up part of the broken glass, raised it, ready to strike. Someone got me in a headlock, pulled me away.

"I'm going to fucking kill him." I tried to fight them off, but there were two of them in front of me, faces I almost recognized, one still behind, dragging me away, sirens wailing, blue lights…

"Adam!"

Blood. So much fucking blood.

"Adam!"

***

"Mr. Brooks."

The voices, like the faces, were familiar.

"Solomon?"

"Hm?"

"I need to clean your cuts."

"Oh." I looked up and smiled an apology. The nurse held out her gloved hand. I offered my bloodied one. She smiled back at me as she wiped over my palm with gauze. It was cold and wet. I watched it turn pink.

"Do you remember me?" she asked. I nodded.

"You went to school with Claire."

"That's right."

She continued to clean my hand, her mascara-lengthened lashes obscuring her eyes. I wanted to ask about Adam. I knew he was alive. They'd told me that much.

"OK. That's not too bad," she said, twisting my hand this way and that. "I'll get it dressed for you and—"

"Is Adam all right?"

"I'll see what I can find out."

"Thanks."

She covered the cuts across my palm with a large square dressing, securing it with a bandage. It seemed to be taking forever.

"There's a police officer waiting to talk to you. Do you feel up to it?"

Not really, but there was little point in delaying the inevitable.

"Sure," I said.

She left, pulling the curtain closed behind her. I leaned back against the wall, shut my eyes and focused on the white noise of hospital comings and goings, trying not to think about… anything. The curtain runners rattled. I opened my eyes again.

"Mr. Brooks?"

"Yes?"

The police officer remained on his feet next to the bed on which I was sitting. I'd seen him before—small town, small police force.

"We're going to leave your statement for now," he said, sounding sympathetic, which struck me as strange. "However, if you could confirm for me whether the man who assaulted you is the same person who sent the text messages, that would be very helpful."

The man who assaulted me? That wasn't how it happened.

Misinterpreting my lack of response, the officer continued, "He's been implicated in another case we're investigating."

Another case.

"Look, Sol," the officer put his hand on my shoulder, and that was when I remembered. He had been at James's funeral.

"Off the record? The other three individually named him. He's going down for this. I'll make damned sure of it."

"You…you…" I couldn't find the right words to ask what I suspected I already knew—that he was the first officer at the scene of the attack on James. He answered anyway.

"He wouldn't have felt much. He was drunk and they hit him from behind."

Whether it was the truth, or a lie intended to comfort me, I didn't care. I nodded.

"Yes. He sent the text messages."

"Good man. That's all we needed to know. The hospital's discharging him into police custody. We have plenty of witnesses who saw him attack you, and the lab got the little gift he left. We've got him, Sol. You can rest easy."

I put my head in my hands, forgetting about the gashes across my palm. It hurt like hell.

"Thanks," I uttered through my hands and the tears. He lightly squeezed my shoulder. The curtain swished. I was alone again.

***

"Hello, Mr. Brooks."

The voice startled me. I hadn't heard the doctor arrive. He smiled and came closer. From his expression there was no way of telling what kind of news he brought.

"Adam had a collapsed lung, from the force of hitting the table, not from the stab wound, which is good. He's having a little trouble breathing, and he's on oxygen and fluids, but the injury was superficial."

"He's OK?"

"He's fine, but we'll admit him for observation overnight, just to make sure. He's more worried about you than himself." He addressed the nurse, Claire's classmate: "Can you take Mr. Brooks over?"

"Of course, Doctor," she said. He smiled again and left. I took a deep breath, felt myself sag in relief. I was so unbelievably tired.

The nurse gave me a moment to get my head together, and then stood nearby as I slid off the bed. I was a little unsteady, but not too bad, all things considered. As we walked across the accident and emergency department, I noticed two police officers outside one of the side rooms. The nurse leaned close to me and said quietly, "They've just read him his rights."

I was too numb to respond. I still wanted to kill him, but it was no longer red mist. It was cold-blooded, calculated. I could picture him tied to a chair while I beat the shit out of him, almost knocking him unconscious, then hitting him over and over again, until he was black with bruises and sobbing for mercy. I wanted to slash him open. I wanted to throttle him. Sure, I wanted to see the other three rot in hell too, but he had rubbed it in our faces, drinking in the King's Head—Yvonne and Jimmy's home, James's home. He deserved to suffer, to die slowly, begging for his life.

A door opened ahead of me, and I stepped into the room, frozen to the spot by the vision of Adam, in a hospital gown, drip in his arm, oxygen tubes clipped to his septum. He was lying on top of the bed covers and still wearing his socks. Black and yellow socks. He looked quite ridiculous. He was snoozing and hadn't heard me arrive. I walked over and kissed him on the forehead, just as he'd been doing to me for the past few days. He opened his eyes, screwed them up a little to focus and smiled his lopsided smile.

"Hey," he whispered, husky and dry-lipped.

"Hey," I whispered back. I smoothed his hair with my hand. "How are you feeling?"

"Sore, but OK."

I blinked back tears.

"I love you," I said. He nodded.

"I know." He reached up, grimacing with the pain. He brushed his palm against my cheek. "I love you too. It's over now."

His eyes closed again, and at first I thought he'd drifted off to sleep, but then he grabbed me and pulled me tight to him. He tried not to cry because it was clearly hurting him to do so, and ended up laughing at himself, which also hurt. I was crying too, and laughing with him, and we were giggling, interspersed with him gasping, "Ouch!" which just made us do it more—all this with James's murderer a few feet down the corridor. We got it under control again, and I helped Adam sip some water. The pain in his chest was making it hard for him to use his arms.

"I need to pee," he said.

There was a urine bottle on the locker next to the bed. I reached across for it.

"I'm not using that."

"I don't think you've got any choice."

"Drop that cot side for me?"

"Adam…"

"I'm going to piss myself!"

I sighed in exasperation and lowered the cot side. He used me to pull himself up, swearing as he slowly swung his legs off the bed, already struggling to catch his breath.

"No," I said very firmly. "You're using the bottle."

He relented and took it from me. I looked away to give him some privacy. There was a thud as the bottle dropped to the floor. "Fuck's sake," he muttered. I picked up the bottle, passed it to him again, and saw his hands shaking.

"Do you want me to hold it?"

He started to laugh, and I daresay blushed a little.

Between us we freed him from his boxers and he positioned himself, while I held the bottle. I met his gaze. After half a minute or so of trying to relax, the slow stream started. I studied the ceiling, faking modesty, glanced back at him. The peeing stopped.

"I seriously can't do this if you're looking at me," he said.

"I'm not."

"No, but I'm looking at you."

"Well don't. Just concentrate on what you're supposed to be doing."

He shook his head, closed his eyes. Started peeing again. I kissed his cheek.

"Pack it in!"

I grinned, but stopped teasing. He finished for real.

"Thank you," he said.

"Welcome," I replied, holding the three-quarters-full bottle at arm's length, not really sure what to do with it.

"Sol?"

"Yeah?"

"Will you marry me?"

Could it have waited for a better time? When we weren't in a hospital, with me holding a cardboard bottle of his piss, him in stylish NHS gown and bumble bee socks, oxygen tubes stuffed up his nose, IV in his arm? Probably.

If it were anyone but my Captain Impatient.

I shrugged. "Yeah, sure. Why not?"

***

The following morning, Adam was discharged into my care, which was laughable, considering he'd spent the first half of the week looking after me through my mini breakdown. Given his generally excellent health, the doctor said we'd be OK to fly back to Boston on Saturday, as planned, and the police came early to take my statement, giving us two more days to get some rest and recuperate.

Yeah, because that was totally going to happen once people found out we were getting married.

"Married?" my mother said.

I was waiting for, "What, like Elton John?" or some such.

"Yes, Mum."

"Well, I suppose that means you won't catch AIDS."

"Very true," said I. "Wedding rings are more than adequate protection…"

"There's no need to be facetious, Solomon."

I shouldn't mock my poor mother. She adored Freddie Mercury and was devastated when he died of "The AIDS," but for a woman of above average intelligence she could be quite dense at times.

When Adam called his family to tell them, I could hear the shrieks and screams from right across the bar, where I was sitting with Yvonne, stupidly worrying that they wouldn't be pleased for us. Adam hung up and rubbed his ear.

"Dad said, if we want them there, we need to get hitched before 'Siptimba' as he's already got a job lined up."

That gave us less than two months. I really couldn't see how we were going to do it.

Adam continued, "So if we go see the registrar now..."

"Now?"

And that was as much protesting as I got to do, because Adam had a trick up his sleeve, and I do mean exactly that.

"You need to check me out," he said, rolling his T-shirt sleeve up to his shoulder, revealing the tattoo I had noticed the first time we met, when he tried to jump the queue at the store.

"What?"

"Check me out."

"What are you talking about?"

"Scan me."

"Why?"

"Do it!"

"The police have got my phone."

He reached into his back pocket. I thought he was going to give me his phone, but no. This one was brand new.

"I'll need to download an app," I said, taking the phone from him.

"It's on there already."

I tutted and unlocked the screen. By now we had an audience, and it was more than a little embarrassing. I held up the phone, trying to keep the tattooed QR code inside the box on-screen. It wasn't the easiest thing, with Yvonne, Jimmy and the King's Head regulars watching, but after a few failed attempts, the phone bleeped. The browser opened.

"You know overseas data charges..."

"UK network," he pointed out smugly. I was about to argue back that buying me a new phone was still an unnecessary expense, as it might be months before we returned to England for good, but I bit my tongue. I was being obstructive, and he was getting impatient—with due cause, admittedly. Even so, did he really want all these smalltown Yorkshire folk seeing his naked ass on Grindr? I mean, it was a nice ass, and everything...

Oh, but this wasn't Grindr. It was—well, I wasn't really sure what it was.

"What is it?" I asked.
"It's a receipt."
"For?"
"Read it."
I read it. It said:

> On demand, I promise to pay Solomon Brooks the sum of:
>
> - My love forever
> - My lips in his constant service
> - My body for as long as he desires it
> - My support in everything he does
> - My heart for it is already his
> - My life
>
> Signed: *Adam Ashton*
> Love of your *new* life, Captain of your Heart
>
> p.s. Sorry for pushing in.

As George would say, *what a sap!*
"On your knees," I said.
"Huh?"
"You missed something."
He smiled. "You want me to do that here?"
I pretended to weigh it up, laughed and kissed him.
"Let's go blow those clouds away."

Epilogue

My birthday. Thirty-two. Not special, but I was maybe a little more up for celebrating this time around.

Also, James's birthday.

We'd intended to leave home early to avoid hitting rush-hour traffic, but Noah and Matty "slept in"—must've been some pretty energetic dreams they were having, the way the bed was squeaking.

Noah peered through the car's rear window into the trunk—how strange to call it that after six months in England.

"What's with the flower pots?" he asked. Adam shot him a warning glance.

"It's OK," I said. "They're for James's grave, Noah."

"Right." He nodded. "Why?"

Matty lightly slapped Noah's arm.

"I think it's a lovely idea," he said.

Huh. Yeah, well, of course you do.

Adam and I had already done the whole personality analysis on Matty. He was gushy and flamboyant, and reminded me of James. He was overemotional and dependent, and reminded Adam of Bobby. Physically, he was slightly built, around five eight, so incredibly blond that his body fuzz gave him a golden aura, and he wore eyeliner and mascara. He loved romcoms, days spent at the beach or window shopping. And he loved Noah. Possibly Noah loved him, but the jury was still out on that one.

Actually, after seeing Matty without mascara a couple of times, I could understand why he thought it necessary. He looked like he had no eyelashes and his eyes were huge—huger still today, as he was wearing his glasses. Pretty geek. Cute, if you liked that sort of thing, which I may have done, once upon a time…

"You OK, handsome?"

"Yep. You, Cap'n?"

Adam grinned and "accidentally" tried to use my knee to put the car in gear.

"Aww," Matty gushed. Noah huffed. "We should totally have pet names for each other."

"Don't think so."

Yep, that was my brother-in-law, all stoic, masculine and… dismissive. Reminded me of someone I used to know. I'll admit, dredging through it all in my bereavement therapy sessions was tough. All that getting it out in the open bull—it really wasn't me. But I was healing OK, and it helped having Noah around, to remind me of how crappy life was before I faced up to everything. Not that Noah was having to deal with anything close to the hell I'd been through. For that, I was eternally grateful—to James, especially, and to people like Calvin. Looking back now, I could more readily appreciate how much fun it was being with Cal. I'd kind of forgotten that, and it was all down to the timing. Cal left, and then James died, and somehow my brain mashed it all together, so that my grief for James transformed into hate for Calvin. Or so my therapist tells me. Whatever, we were young, and maybe in his own way, Cal loved me, but politics was always his real passion. In fact, I'd seen him on TV a while back, as spokesperson for a charity protesting the FDA ban on organ donation by gay men. He did a great interview—calm, assertive, to the point—I guess we all find our place in the world eventually. Even the stubborn bastards, like me and Noah. Maybe he'd grow out of it. Maybe Matty would stay around long enough to help him, but they were only nineteen. Plenty of life ahead of them yet.

We set off on the three-and-a-half-hour drive from Norfolk to Yorkshire (like it was going to take anywhere near that long with who was behind the wheel), and I tuned out from Matty's chattering, listening instead to the radio, thinking ahead to the party. James had died the summer before we turned twenty-one—the real reason I'd gone to the States and decided to stay there—and I'd never celebrated a birthday since. Until the ton of daffodils Adam had filled my office with last year, the only way I knew it was my birthday at all was the annual phone call from my mother and gift from Elise—always cufflinks. Last year's were plain black with white lettering, both bearing the words, "Thirty something." In my collection I also had: "Trust me/I'm an engineer," "CTRL/ESC," "If found/return to wife," as well as X-Wing fighters and a miniature protractor and set square. Predictable, yes, but both functional and gift-like—perfect for someone like me, not to mention giving Elise the chance to make her point, while also crippling my defense by turning it into ingratitude. Oh, she wasn't that bad really, and she had sent me love and best wishes.

So a birthday party, then, of sorts. It was actually more a celebration of James's life, and of justice finally being served, with the four men who killed him sentenced to life imprisonment. To my mind it was nowhere near enough, and in my darker moments the vengeful demon would rise from deep within, bringing with him heinous twisted visions of cruel retribution that frankly made me no better than them. Hate is bleak, and it destroys you. Whenever it threatened to take me over, I'd remind myself of what Yvonne said—about it fading eventually. I found some solace in that. But mostly I chose not to think about them. These days, I'd only realize I was thinking about them because I hadn't been, if that makes any sense at all. Probably not. It had been a crazy year—in a good way. The best of my life, so far... We'd moved back to England, into that big old farmhouse. And it really was way too big for just the three of us, so, we thought, why not rent out a couple of rooms to students? It worked right up to the point of, "Matty, this is Noah."

And we'd got married last summer. George flew over for the wedding, stayed at the King's Head, along with the Ashtons, which was also where we had our reception. George thought it was quaint. George thought everything "British" was quaint, including my mother, whom she patted on the arm at frequent intervals, telling her she was "a hoot." She took it well.

"Is everyone in Boston gay, Solomon?"

"No, Mum. Why?"

"She keeps touching me."

"She's just being friendly."

"And she has a man's name."

Conclusive, no?

I zoned back in to the sound of Freddie Mercury's soaring vocals coming through the car speakers. Adam and I glanced at each other, held our laughter right through to the opera section, at which point it exploded from us, leaving our backseat companions somewhat bemused. Sorry guys, private joke.

***

The bitter blast from the North Sea speared our faces like shards of ice as we made our way through the cemetery. In spite of the cold, it was beautiful, with mounds of snowdrops huddling in the shelter of willows, bare but for the green floret shoots of new leaves. Purple, white and yellow crocuses brashly lined the path ahead, quivering rows of tiny hot air balloons readying for takeoff. And there were daffodils, of course, various and abundant. Adam squeezed my hand, that unspoken, *You OK?* I squeezed back. *Yes.* I was.

Today, as always, James's grave was adorned with seasonal flowers of every color. I set down the pot I was carrying. Adam did the same.

"Don't you feel a bit weird, digging in a grave?" Matty asked, passing me the trowel. I smiled.

"He's buried a bit deeper, Matt," I said. He rolled those huge eyes of his.

"You know what I mean."

I did, and he was right. I was feeling very uneasy, standing over the place where James lay at rest, moving aside other people's floral offerings. A random and wholly inappropriate thought entered my head—Donny's question. I peered down at the space I'd just cleared. *Definitely a top today, what with you all the way down there.*

I knelt on the cold earth and prodded into it with my trowel, removing a tiny mound of soil, recalling the countless times I'd seen my mother preparing our garden for new plants.

"The compost is still in the car."

"I'll go get it," Adam said. He left. Noah and Matty loitered. I carried on digging.

"Hey there, blue skies. How's heaven treating you?"

"Oh, you know. It's OK."

"Only OK?"

"It's a bit boring. I mean, look at the place, won't you? There's no bedrooms to tidy, no chores to do, no parents hassling…"

"But you're free."

"I can do whatever I like, go wherever I choose, be here, there, and everywhere, all at once. But it's not quite being alive, is it?"

"Don't say that."

"It's true. Living is better. But you don't need me dragging you down, not today. It's our birthday. And I hear you got married."

"I did. His name's Adam. I think you'd like him."

"He makes you happy."

"Yeah."

"Then I already do."

"I wish you could've met him."

"Me too."

"I'm sorry I let you down. I hope you can forgive me."

"You didn't let me down, sunshine, but if you need it, my forgiveness is yours. Just be happy and forgive yourself."

"I'm getting there."

"Yeah, you are. Hey, guess what? Your husband's back."

Adam crouched beside me and tipped a little of the compost into the two holes I had made. I carefully removed the soil plugs from each plant pot and positioned them, patting the earth flat around the new shoots of daffodils. A little gasp sounded behind us. Adam chuckled.

"Matty?" I guessed.

"How did you know?"

Adam held out his hand to me, helping me to my feet. The knees of my jeans were soaked wet through, yet I didn't feel cold, with my captain's warm strong arms around me, holding me close, holding me together. We stepped back to admire the daffodils we had planted, that would return each spring, to bloom for James's and my birthday. I snuggled up to Adam.

"You ready?" he asked. I nodded, took one last look at James's photo.

"Happy birthday, blues skies," I whispered.

And the wind whispered back.

"Happy birthday, my sweet sunshine."

The End

About the Author

Debbie McGowan is an author and publisher based in a semi-rural corner of Lancashire, England. She writes character-driven, realist fiction, celebrating life, love and relationships. A working class girl, she 'ran away' to London at seventeen, was homeless, unemployed and then homeless again, interspersed with animal rights activism (all legal, honest ;)) and volunteer work as a mental health advocate. At twenty-five, she went back to college to study social science—tough with two toddlers, but they had a stay-at-home dad, so it worked itself out. These days, the toddlers are young women, and Debbie teaches undergraduate students, writes novels and runs an independent publishing company, occasionally grabbing an hour of sleep where she can.

Social Media Links

Website: debbiemcgowan.co.uk
Newsletter Signup: eepurl.com/b8emHL
Blog: deb248211.blogspot.com
Facebook: facebook.com/DebbieMcGowanAuthor and facebook.com/beatentrackpublishing
Twitter: @writerdebmcg
YouTube: youtube.com/deb248211
Instagram: instagram/writerdebmcg
Google+: plus.google.com/+DebbieMcGowan
Tumblr: writerdebmcg.tumblr.com
LinkedIn: uk.linkedin.com/in/writerdebmcg
Goodreads: goodreads.com/DebbieMcGowan

By the Author

Checking Him Out Series
Checking Him Out (Book One)
Checking Him Out For the Holidays (Novella)
Hiding Out (Novella – Noah and Matty – HBTC Crossover)
Taking Him On (Book Two – Noah and Matty)
Checking In (Book Three)
The Making of Us (Book Four – Jesse and Leigh)

Seeds of Tyrone Series
~ co-written with Raine O'Tierney
Leaving Flowers (Book One)
Where the Grass is Greener (Book Two)
Christmas Craic and Mistletoe (Book Three)

Hiding Behind The Couch Series
The ongoing story of 'The Circle'…
Nine friends from high school;
Nine friends for life.

The Story So Far…
in chronological order:
novellas and short novels are 'stand-alone' stories, but tie in with the series. Think Middle Earth—well, more Middle England, but with a social conscience!

Beginnings (Novella)
Ruminations (Novel)
Class-A (Short Story)
Hiding Behind The Couch (Season One)
No Time Like The Present (Season Two)
The Harder They Fall (Season Three)

Crying in the Rain (Novel)
First Christmas (Novella)
In The Stars Part I: Capricorn–Gemini (Season Four)
Breaking Waves (Novella)
In The Stars Part II: Cancer–Sagittarius (Season Five)
A Midnight Clear (Novella)
Red Hot Christmas (Novella)
Two By Two (Season Six)
Hiding Out (Novella – CHO Crossover)
Breakfast at Cordelia's Aquarium (Short Story)
Chain of Secrets (Novella)
Those Jeffries Boys (Novel)
The WAG and The Scoundrel (Gray Fisher #1)
Reunions (Season Seven)
To Be Sure (Novella)
Tabula Rasa (Gray Fisher #2)
What A Scorcher! (Short Story)
Goth of Christmas Past (Novel)

Stand-Alone Stories

Champagne (LGBT Historical Novel)
'Time to Go' in *Story Salon Big Book of Stories* (Contemporary Short Story)
And The Walls Came Tumbling Down (Sci-fi Novel)
No Dice (Sci-fi Novel)
Double Six (Sci-fi Novel)
Sugar and Sawdust (M/M Romance Short Story)
Cherry Pop Valentine (M/M Romance Short Story)
Coming Up ~ co-written with Al Stewart (LGBT Short Story)
Of the Bauble (LGBT Fantasy Romance Novella)
So Long, Little Black Diamonds (Short (True) Story)
The Pastor's Last Drop (Historical Novel (Ongoing) – Wattpad)
When Skies Have Fallen (LGBT Historical Romance Novel)
A Snowy Ball (When Skies Have Fallen #1.5)
The Great Village Bun Fight (Contemporary Novella)

www.hidingbehindthecouch.com
www.debbiemcgowan.co.uk

Beaten Track Publishing

For more titles from Beaten Track Publishing,
please visit our website:

http://www.beatentrackpublishing.com

Thanks for reading!

Made in the USA
Middletown, DE
19 September 2019